DECEPTION

BY

NIGHTFALL

BY

S. L. MCMULLIN

Book 3 in the *Secrets by Moonlight* saga

Special Thanks

to my husband for making all those special trips to the convenient store on my behalf to retrieve a much needed pick-me-up that not only gave me clarity of mind while spending hours upon hours writing and editing this book, but also helped me stay alert long into the night to meet my writing goals as a busy mother of four. My sanity thanks you. Immensely!

Thank you to my daughter, Jenna, for being my sounding board. And, of course, to all my children for continuing to understand the importance of my work and your willingness to *'disappear'* for a bit so I can get it done.

TABLE OF CONTENTS

Also by S. L. McMullin

SECRETS BY MOONLIGHT

FATE BY SUNRISE

Deception
by
Nightfall

By S. L. McMullin

R & S Publishing

CHAPTER 1

Deception and Lies

With his brow creased into a deep vee, Niall looks at Finn. "We can't just go! Not without a plan or something!"

"Then figure it out!" Finn growls. When Marcas eyes him keenly, he turns away.

"Where do we even start? Conall keeps moving hideouts. Too many trails to follow. Not enough people!" Sam says.

"I'll take Sam and Finn and head back to the shop. See if whoever took Jamie left something behind. A scent or trail, maybe," Korin says.

"Good. Then Niall and I will check out Conall's last known location. His heightened sense of smell may find something we've missed. Hopefully, it will lead us in the right direction. Anyone seen Tate?"

"Not since this morning." Sam shrugs.

"No," Korin and Niall affirm.

"I did!" Ardan says. "Down by the candy shop earlier. Ten-thirty, ten-forty-five, maybe. He ducked behind the building."

"You're sure?" Marcas eyes Korin. "Why would he—"

"To take Jamie, of course!" Ardan grunts. "He's betrayed us all! Ran off to join Conall."

"He wouldn't, would he?" Niall asks.

"The hell he wouldn't!" Ardan retorts.

"We don't know that. Being in town could be coincidental and nothing more," Marcas warns.

"You and I know he's more than capable of something like this!" Ardan says to Korin. "He was there. I saw him. He's the only one!"

"It'll have to wait." Taking my hand, Marcas pulls me upright, a frown of worry on his lips. "We need to go, Shae. It will be best if you stay here with Ardan."

"What? No! I want to go with you! Don't you dare leave me here with him!"

Ardan's face sinks. "Please, let me help. I swear, I'll keep you safe."

Pulling me close, Marcas hugs me. I try to resist, but his firm, yet gentle arms won't allow it. "Please, Shae. There's no one else. He's hurt and will only slow us down. I need everyone searching."

With tears streaking down my cheeks, I scowl at Marcas. "You better know what you're doing." He kisses me tenderly, making me falter. "Hurry, please." I say somberly, knowing he's right. We'd only complicate things by going.

"Let's move," Korin orders. Sam and Finn follow him. Having passed the barrier, they change into their wolf form and rush into the dense trees.

"Ardan, never out of your sight!" Marcas orders over my head, then he looks at me. "I promise I'll bring Jamie back." Hugging me, he whispers in my ear, "If Tate shows up—" Then he stares at me as if to relay a hidden message of warning. "I don't know what's going on, but things don't add up." Using his normal voice again, he says, "Keep to the house, and whatever happens, don't leave the yard."

"On my honor." Ardan bows with his hand fisted to his chest.

"I won't," I say, and then Marcas kisses me once more before moving to the protective barrier.

Mid-stride, his body begins to transform. The familiar blackish-gray fur travels down the length of his body. His arms and legs morph until he becomes the same majestic creature who had saved me in the forest once before.

At the tree's edge, he looks back at me. His large eyes shimmer in the sun, full of angst for what I assume is having to leave me in someone else's care once again. Captivated by his splendor, I watch him through my tears and wave. Letting out a slight whimper, he then barks twice before turning and sprinting into the woods.

"We'll get her back, Shae. I promise," Niall says, then he runs and transforms, as Marcas and the others had, before he disappears behind a tuft of large pine trees.

I wrap my arms around myself. Cold and alone, I try to keep from falling apart as I stare at the spot where everyone else has gone.

"We should go inside," Ardan says, motioning toward the stairs.

Shaking my head rigidly, I remain where I stand, unwilling to budge for the likes of him—the one who let Jamie be taken.

"If I'm to protect you, you must trust me."

"Well, I don't!"

"Shae, it wasn't my fault! I was hit from behind—no time to react. I swear, this is all Tate's doing."

How can he think such a thing? Other than seeing Tate in town, what proof does he have that he did this? Could he really be capable of such a heinous show of treachery?

"Marcas is right. Being in town doesn't make Tate capable of doing something like this."

"No, but his maliciousness does." Ardan gives a snide snort. "I mean, you saw how he acted this morning!"

"He was only trying to get in the heads of our enemies. Then you go and attack him for it!"

"Like-minded with our enemy is treachery at its finest."

"Thinking differently than you doesn't make him our enemy."

"In my book, it's the defining action!" he says with a leer.

"But he's your brother!"

"No, he's not." His eyes shift, heavy with loathing. "Hasn't been for a *very* long time. I can't believe you, of all people, would stand up for him! I dare say you've been made a fool, Shae."

"What's that supposed to mean?"

"You haven't seen how he looks at you? The constant disgust in his eyes? He detests you, Shae. I can't be the only one who's seen it."

My stomach lurches, sinking like a heavy rock. I had seen it. There's no denying it. But our last conversation was different. A connection was made—a glimpse of the real Tate shining through.

Not this hideous, heartless, loathsome person Ardan now tries to paint him to be.

"No. It's obvious he doesn't want to be here and detests you, but what reason would he have to hate me?"

"For the sheer fun of it? He's bored, and it's something to pass the time."

Tate's hostile expression, which I had seen the other day through the window, flashes into my mind. Was it proof of hatred or his annoyance with everyone and everything peeking through?

"It wouldn't surprise me if he traded sides just to see you in misery when Conall captures you."

My insides shudder at the conviction of Ardan's statement. "You're wrong! What about at Duke's? He tried to warn me!"

Ardan laughs. "Mind games. He's exceptionally good at them. Made you believe in just one moment of concern that he genuinely cared."

Could he be that good an actor? To be so heartless and evil as to hide such loathing from me in conversation?

"Even so, why throw everything away? Turn his back on his family just because he can't stand me! Why?"

"All is fair in love and revenge. What better way to rid oneself of their wretched family than to let your enemy do it for you? I'm afraid you're only a means to that end for him."

"No! He's not like that!"

"Are you willing to bet your life on it, Shae?" Ardan's eyes narrow. "Jamie's life, perhaps?"

My heart patters—my answer, uncertain. "But he would never betray—"

"If you think that, then you don't know him as well as you think you do."

"That's funny; he said the same thing about you!"

"See what I mean? All lies."

In frustration, I turn away from Ardan. "He's unhappy with a lot of things, but that doesn't mean he would give Jamie to my enemy just to torment me. I can't believe someone to be so evil."

"Believe what you want, girly, but my bet's on him. Regardless of his reasons, he's doing it, and I'm going to be the one to stop him!"

Right on cue, Tate rounds the corner of the house, emerging from under the stairs. His eyes are puffy and bloodshot.

I freeze.

"Hey," he says sullenly as he walks up to me. "Where'd everyone go?"

"Don't play stupid. You know damn well where they went!" Ardan steps toward him, his hurt leg dragging.

"I wasn't talking to you, Ardan, so butt out!" Tate says, his jaw clenched. "Shae, what's going on?" He steps toward me, and I move back. "Wh-Why do you pull away? You're . . . afraid of me?"

"Jamie was taken outside the shop today." Hot tears fall down my cheeks. I swipe them away aggressively.

"And you think I had something to do with it? I'm angry, not stupid. I would never betray any of you. I-I wouldn't do that to you."

"I just . . . I don't know—"

"Who was there? Stood watch?"

My eyes shift toward Ardan.

"Huh, isn't that somethin'? Someone finally bested you, eh, big shot?" Tate says with a hint of gladness.

"Drop the act, Tate!" Ardan yells as he comes to me. "No one's buying it, including Shae. Your plan to get close to her failed."

"Why don't you shut your damn mouth, Ardan! I said I didn't do it! Please, Shae, don't listen to him. I don't hate you!"

"I saw you in town; I know it was you!"

"You lie! I was there," Tate points to the forest behind the house, "by the river!"

"Convenient. Truly. To be somewhere no one saw you, nor can vouch for your whereabouts. Smart call!

The only thing is, I saw you. You can't lie yourself out of that, can you?"

Tate lowers his hand to his side as his fingers clench into a fist. Several knuckles pop. Glaring hard at Ardan, he then looks at me. "Tell me you don't believe this jerk. I thought you could see through all that. I'm not a traitor!" His eyes glaze over with tears, frustration and anger rippling through them.

My head is spinning. Who to trust? Who? Make this nightmare go away!

"Why didn't you come?" I say more as a wonder than an accusation.

Tate blinks. "I-I heard, I just—"

"Needed more time to get back from stealing Jamie?" Ardan huffs.

"No!" Tate then sighs. "I needed a minute."

When he looks at me, I see no malice or hint of deception within his eyes, only pleading sorrow. And yet, do I know him? Can I trust myself to recognize a lie when it's happening in front of me?

"Come on, don't give in to his sappy, fake puppy dog pout, Shae. Just let me at him! Be done with this." Ardan moves to grab Tate, who adjusts his weight onto his back leg, arms lifted, ready to strike.

"No, Ardan," I say, forcing him back. "Just let me . . . let me think."

Ardan glowers loathingly at Tate, clenching his jaw. Tate stays still, his eyes locked on mine.

"Please," Tate whispers, his eyes begging me. "Can't you see what he's doing? Feeding you lies. Making you doubt me—not trust me—when it's *him* you can't trust. Have I ever-*ever* given you a reason to doubt me? Remember our first conversation? Things aren't always what they seem, Shae. Please trust that if nothing else!"

"I-I can't—" My brain pounds with muddied confusion. I take a step back from them, my eyes shifting from one to the other.

I've seen glimpses of Tate's compassion and sincere distress for my well-being. But I don't know if they are real, even with his current protests to tempt me.

"It's not going to work, Tate. You can snivel and cry all you want, but no one'll believe you, including her!"

"Ardan, I'm warning you. I mean it, *shut up*!" Tate roars.

Unsure who to believe, I take another step away from them. Then another.

"No, Shae, wait! Listen-listen!" Tate says, stepping toward me, but Ardan blocks him. "Think for a second. Ardan's supposed to be protecting Jamie, right? This mighty man, all-powerful, and yet someone bested him? Impossible, right?"

"You're such a punk! You jumped me from behind. I didn't have time to react," Ardan says through clenched teeth as he goes to shove Tate, but Tate stumbles back, out of reach.

"Oh, right, and suddenly, I have what it takes to beat you? Hold on, let me get my phone out so I can record you saying that!"

"Stop it!" My voice echoes back off the house at us. "I can't think with the two of you arguing."

Ardan huffs. "What's to think about?"

Too much! Think, Shae, think! What doesn't add up? Think!

"You know, as well as I do, he's a liar and a no good..."

Ardan is ginormous and unrelentingly boastful of how strong he is. How could Tate, let alone anyone, take him down with one hit? "Not possible," I mutter under my breath.

"Oh, believe it! Ain't worth the ground he stands on." Ardan scowls.

"Why don't you come over here and say it to my face?"

"You'd like that, wouldn't you? You need a good—"

"How?" I ask. "How did you not see Tate coming?"

"What?" Ardan stops short.

"You saw him before. Had your suspicions about him. Why not be on your guard then?" I say, shifting my weight as I step away from him.

Ardan's eyes go ablaze as they shoot from me to Tate, then back again. "I already told you! He was—I—"

"And when you came to, you didn't think to call Marcas?" I prod further.

"Yeah, seems odd, don't you think? It'd be the first thing I'd've done." Tate scoffs.

Giving an evil eye as steely and dangerous as his fists, Ardan snarls. "I already told you; my phone was taken. I came as fast as I could. My leg—"

"There had to have been a phone somewhere. Someone walking by, in a store, maybe?" Tate interrogates deeper. "Guess no numbers memorized then, huh, mate?"

"Shut up!" Ardan's nose flares as he moves forward on his now solid, seemingly uninjured leg.

No pain?

"Your leg—tell me, how did you hurt it again?" I ask, making him stop short.

He steps off it and winces. "Must've been from the attack. My head—still hard to remember what happened."

"Well, which is it? One punch from me and you're down, or a brawl? I'd like to think if it were me, I'd remember a fight against a meager opponent such as myself if I had lost said fight."

"I don't have to justify anything! Marcas and Korin believe me, so what does it matter to you?"

"Because you're obviously lying!" Tate grunts. "Can't keep your story straight, can ya?"

Ardan roars with a fiery rage and charges Tate, who tries to punch back. Ardan sees it and dodges to the side, countering with a punch to Tate's jaw, snapping his head to one side.

"Ardan, stop!" I scream, but Ardan keeps throwing punches, managing one more connection with Tate's cheek. Without flinching, Tate throws his fist, hitting Ardan square in the chin, then raises his hand to strike again.

"Stop it!" I holler again so intensely that my throat burns.

Tate and Ardan push off each other, creating a large triangle with me as one of the corners. Their hair is disheveled. A scarlet drop of blood drips from Tate's cut lip. He wipes it away with the sleeve of his shirt.

"Now, do you believe me?" Ardan says, taking in a heaping lungful of air. "He's rotten to the core."

"Go'da hell!" Tate counters while bent over with his hands on his knees.

"I can't—" The wheels in my head are turning so fast that I can't keep hold of a thought before the next one comes. "I don't—"

Ardan's desperate to pin everything on Tate and refuses to explain the discrepancies in his story. Why? Why accuse Tate of such a thing? Kidnapping? Can it be true? Not only that, Ardan has belittled and said downright awful things about Tate's character, even when I've been witness to the contrary. From Tate's own words, I have heard the level of hatred they have for one another. Yet it's one's word against the other. The only proof Ardan has of Tate's involvement is seeing him in town, which Tate ultimately denies having been. How am I to know the truth?

"Shae, come on! No time left. Let's take him out!" Ardan grumbles. "Before it's too late."

Glancing up to the big windows on the deck, I see Tax propped up on the windowsill, staring back at me. An unsettling feeling weighs me down. Stuck inside, he cannot protect me if I choose wrong.

Shaking the thought away, I look back and forth between Ardan and Tate, my mind screaming, *'think!'* as I take a step away.

But if Tate wasn't there, why would Ardan insist he was? To make him the fall guy?

Tate was right about one thing. A bump on the head would never knock Ardan out cold. Then again, Tate could have had help.

My heart is racing. Which one of them do I trust? Who is telling me the truth, and who only tells me what I want to hear?

My stomach flops as I feel the magnitude of my choice. I don't want to be wrong. No! I *can't* be wrong!

Looking at Tate, I see his pleading eyes so full of child-like fear and sadness looking back at me; innocent and misunderstood. Not the face of a monster. Not like Ardan's distorted, rage-filled features.

But why go through all the trouble to blame Tate if it wasn't him who took Jamie?

Understanding suddenly aligns in my mind, the last puzzle piece fitting into place. Ardan wants Tate out. Out of the family. Out of commission indefinitely!

"Lies," I whisper aloud to myself. "All lies."

"Right!" Ardan hisses. "Now you see."

"I do," I say, narrowing my eyes on Ardan. "I see everything!" When Ardan grabs for Tate, I add, "I see you despise Tate!"

Ardan stops. "Not really a news flash, now, is it?"

"I see your relentless attempt to place Tate in town. To make Marcas and Korin believe him capable of taking Jamie."

Slowly, Tate and I move away from Ardan, closing the gap between us.

"Don't be a fool. You're playing right into his hands!"

"You know, I don't think I am. I believe you want me to think that Ardan, but I don't."

"You-you're going to side with that, that piece of crap? That delinquent!"

"Because I know Tate didn't do it." The moment the words leave my lips, I am as sure of them as I've ever been.

When Tate reaches me, a warm smile shines at me, and I know he is irrevocably free of Ardan's stifling grip.

"Go ahead then. Get yourself killed! What do I care? It's not like it's the end of Marcas' reign or anything."

"Says you," I snap back. "But I can't figure out why you'd lie."

"Because he's with Conall," Tate says with loathing as he moves in front to protect me, his hands raised in fists.

"Wh-What?"

A sinister leer widens on Ardan's face. "Never pinned you for smart. What gave it away?"

"Call it a hunch. Explains why you weren't upset like the rest of us when Tavis showed up at the bar."

"Because I told him she'd be there. Sam was so easy to manipulate. The idiot probably thinks it was his idea. You're in so far over your head, it's not even funny. There's nowhere to hide. Conall always gets what he wants."

"With Conall?" I breathe. "No!" No! No, this can't be. Ardan hates Tate—yes. Pines for Jamie—double yes. But willing to put her in danger? Betray everyone? How could he do that?

"I knew you were a manipulative piece of crap, but this?" Tate says.

"Oh, but you made it so easy, Tate. Years and years of insubordinate behavior. Of course, Marcas and Korin would believe me over you."

"You had everything! Dad's love. Korin's approval! And you throw it all away. For what? To become one of Conall's brown-nosing minions? What?"

"When will you realize there's so much more than the mundane, ritualistic life waiting for you back home? Korin might be ridiculous enough for it, but not me. I have big plans, and Conall promises to make them happen.

Though I admit, when he first contacted me, I didn't think it was worth my while. But after coming and seeing for myself, I couldn't allow an offer like his to go to waste. Not when the riches are so inviting."

"What could he possibly promise you to make you choose him over your own family?" I ask.

"Oh, quite a few things, actually. But the last—now that's the keeper." He grins with a crooked sneer. "He gets the girl—I get the girl."

"What?" I growl.

"He means Jamie." Tate grunts. "She's for him when he delivers you."

"Are you serious?" I scream, lunging toward him, but Tate holds me back. "Can't get her on your own, so you kidnap her? You disgust me," I say through clenched teeth. "If you think Jamie will let you—"

"She won't have a choice. Conall guarantees it." Ardan's words drift off his tongue like hot ice, setting my nerves on fire as a chill of dread threatens to do me in.

"I won't let that happen!" Tate says, the conviction in his tone resonating through me. If ever I doubted his fortitude to stand up to Ardan, I don't now.

"You? The biggest weakling of the bunch. You're gonna stop it?" Ardan laughs snidely. "You've never even seen a day of battle in your life. You're as good as dead if you go up against any of the wolves Conall has in his back pocket. You all are if you try to keep him from what he wants." Then he grins at me. "Oh, but girly, does he have great plans for you!"

"I don't care what he wants!" I say, feeling sick to my stomach. Conall thinks he can control me?

"Enough!" Ardan bellows. "I leave you with a message. A warning, Shae, I suggest you heed. You have until this time tomorrow to come willingly, or we'll attack and take you by force. To be clear, we don't intend to leave any survivors. Come without protest and sacrifice yourself for those you love or die along with them. Your choice."

"Never!" I say with contempt.

"I won't let you get away with it!" Tate switches his weight onto his back foot. "I'll fight till the death if I have to."

"Oh, I'm counting on it, little brother." A cold, dark scowl shadows Ardan's eyes as he steps back.

As Tate moves, he extends his arm, ready to snag Ardan. "Shae will never be with Conall, and we will get Jamie back. If you—"

"Conall *will* succeed—one way or another. And those of you hell-bent on continuing the idiotic traditions of our forebears will perish, along with *anyone* sharing the same stale values." Ardan quickly glances at the trees and then at us. "Oh, and Tate? Make no mistake, I'll take immense pleasure in watching you die a long, *painful* death."

No matter how many strides Tate takes to get to Ardan, he's still too far away to get him.

"I suggest you decide before it's too late." Then Ardan turns and runs across the yard and into the thick trees.

Tate leaps to follow, but I tug his arm. "Tate, don't. Let him go."

"But I can follow; see where he goes!"

"What if it's what he wants? You can't leave me here unprotected. And even if I went with you, I can't change into a wolf yet. No way could I keep up."

"You're right, I'm sorry." He takes a long breath. "I can't believe he's with Conall. I hate his guts, but still."

"You had no idea?"

"He's a dick and makes my life a living hell, but no. Not until you made me realize there was no other explanation for him needing me to take the blame this time."

"We have to tell the others!"

"No! I mean, he's Korin's number one and their friend. They won't believe he'd betray them. They'll think I did something to him."

"Tate, we don't have a choice. We can't waste any more time!"

Giving a nod, Tate reaches for his phone, but mine rings first. *'Marge-Jamie's boss'* shows up on the screen. A cold sweat breaks out over my body as I gulp down hard. How am I going to lie to her, believably?

Mouthing *'hold on'* to Tate, I say, "Hello," while we move to the chairs under the deck.

"Shae, it's Marge. Have you seen Jamie?" Her voice carries a hint of frustration, underlined with worry.

"Uh . . . yes. Shoot, I'm sorry, I, uh . . . I was gonna call you. Jamie threw up all over herself and had to go home. She told me to call you, but I forgot. I'm so sorry for making you worry."

"No, it's fine." Irritation stirs in her tone. "I just wished she'd let Nancy know before leaving like that."

"She said there wasn't time. I guess it was pretty bad."

"All right, then, maybe I'll give her a call and see how she's doing."

"No! I mean, you don't have to do that. I just checked on her, and she's kind of out of it. Nasty thing, the flu."

"Oh, umm . . . ok, well, thanks. Let me know if she needs anything." Then she hangs up.

I look at Tate and take a heavy breath. He presses a button on his screen and then places the phone between our heads. Ringing sounds through its speaker.

"Tate?" Korin's voice booms through.

"Yes. Korin, listen, come quick. Something's happened and—"

"Where are you?" he asks, an edge to his tone.

"I'm with Shae at the house."

Silence.

Tate eyes me as he grips the phone, his hand slightly shaking. "Korin? Did you hear me?"

"Shae's with you?" Korin asks, his voice rigid. "Where's Ardan?"

"He took off. Look, we'll explain when you get here. Is Marcas with you?"

"He just left. He wanted to check on something before heading back to the house. I was about to follow. We're a few minutes out." Loud, rustling noises come through. "Can I talk to Shae for a moment?"

Tate looks at me with an *'I told you so'* expression prominent on his face.

"Korin, I'm here," I say, leaning close to the phone. "You're on speaker."

Another long pause.

"Korin, please, come quick! We have a message from Conall."

When Korin doesn't reply, Tate grabs my hand, his touch as cold as ice.

"Korin?" I say again.

"We're on our way," Korin says in a rush, followed by a loud click. The phone's screen fades to black.

CHAPTER 2

The Hard Road

Korin sprints across the yard, a look of determination on his face. "Where's Ardan?"

"See, I told you," Tate grumbles, standing up.

"He'll listen. It'll be okay." Though the look on Korin's face gives me doubt.

"Where is he?" Colliding with Tate, Korin's forearm bulges as he grips him and shoves him up against the deck post. "What did you do with him?"

"Nothing!"

"Korin, stop!" I try to tug him away from Tate, but his hold is firm. "Tate didn't do anything. Let us explain!"

Using his body, Korin shoves me, sending me toppling to the ground. I get up but remain at a distance. This is between them now.

"Get off me!" Tate grunts, struggling to break free. "Listen? Yeah, right!"

"Tell me now! That's an order!"

Through gritted teeth, Tate snarls, "Not without Marcas," as he claws at Korin's arm, pressing on his upper chest.

"Now!"

Breathing rapidly, his nose flaring, Tate lets his hands drop. His narrowing, rigid eyes glare Korin down.

Korin releases a rumbling growl that echoes off the house, then punches the wood above Tate's head. Tate doesn't flinch an inch; however, I trip over my feet, stumbling back.

Inside the house, Tax barks wildly, his front paws dancing along the windowsill.

Marcas, Niall, Sam, and Finn sprint through the trees and into the yard in human form.

Marcas wraps his arm around my waist, pulling me toward the center of the field. "Are you hurt?" he asks in a panic.

Shaking my head fervently, I point to Korin and Tate. "Please, Marcas!"

"Watch her," he says to Niall before running toward the deck.

"What's happened? Why are they fighting?" Niall asks. But my focus is on Korin and Tate.

"Korin, enough. Let him speak," Marcas says, rushing up on them.

Korin's eyes are thin slits as he glares at Tate, still gripped in his muscular stronghold.

Extending a firm hand, Marcas puts it on Korin's shoulder. He jerks his head toward Marcas, his eyes burning with wrath. "I need to know what happened!"

"Okay," Marcas says calmly. "Then maybe let him go so we can find out."

Korin shoves Tate to the side as he steps away. Catching his footing, Tate rights himself and huffs, rubbing where Korin's fingers had dug into his skin. I try to run to him, but Niall grabs my arm, holding me back.

"Niall, please!" I beg.

After a moment, he nods then releases me, and I run to Tate.

"You good?" I ask him. He nods once, though the look in his eyes tells me he's anything but fine. How can he be? His brother practically beat him.

"You want to know what happened to Ardan?" Tate says, glaring at Korin. "Well, I'll tell you. Your golden boy decided life would be better with Conall than with his own damn family, that's what! And his reward? Jamie!"

"What did you just say?" Finn gasps.

25

"Ardan took Jamie?" Niall adds.

Sam grunts. "That's not right!"

"He said you did!" Finn says, pointing his finger at Tate.

"What proof do you have?" Korin yells.

"Besides the present his fist gave my face? Why don't you ask Shae? She was there."

They all look at me with skepticism. Marcas moves closer to me. I assume it's to get me out of harm's way should things get out of hand. But then again, he may only want to comfort me.

"It's true," I say, then clear my throat. "I heard Ardan myself. He's with Conall. And he took Jamie." As I confirm it aloud, my heart aches. Even if Ardan is a traitor and a horrible person, he is still their friend and Korin's brother.

"No, no way. This can't be." Sam looks at the others, his eyes wide. "We've been friends since forever. He'd never do anything like this."

Korin shakes his head. "No! I can't—I won't believe it!"

"Don't you get it? He played us all. Wants you to think it's impossible. For decades, he's been pitting everyone against me, undercutting me every chance he gets. And you and father believed every bit of it!" Tate says acidly. For a moment, he clenches his eyes shut as though trying to hold back rage from years and years of heartache, torment, and misery.

Gradually, they open again. "And here we are again," he mumbles more poignantly than snidely.

"You expect me to believe my most loyal soldier is capable of treason?" Korin says sharply. "No!"

"Oh, get over yourself. And stop idolizing him. See him for what he really is: a liar and a traitor! Whatever. Don't believe me. But if I hadn't come back when I did, Shae would've been taken too, and that's a fact! She's safe, and he's gone for good!"

Korin looks at me, desperate for me to deny it. I faintly shake my head, my forehead creased. "I'm sorry, Korin."

His eyes shift from an angry glare to pensive perplexity. Then his features harden as he glares into the woods past us. I have no idea if he believes me, but it was worth a shot.

It makes me sick to think of how much Ardan's betrayal has hurt everyone around me. I wish I could set back time. Change the fates. Right this devastating wrong. But if I've learned anything these past few months, it's that with the life-altering bad comes the unexpected good. Eventually. Though, I don't see what good could come of such wicked abandonment.

I look at Tate. His body is stiff as he stares unwaveringly at Korin. Slipping my hand into his, I give a squeeze. For a second, he grins, but it vanishes when Korin looks back at him. Straightening up, Tate releases my hand and steps forward.

"I'm not the enemy here, Korin. Never was."

"I've been a fool," Korin says calmly, all anger gone. "To ask for trust and loyalty, yet not to give it in return. I should have—"

"Wouldn't've made a difference. Neither of us would have ever seen this coming, even if Ardan hadn't done what he did to me."

"I'm so sorry, my brother." Korin bows.

Tate purses his lips and mimics Korin's reverence. "Siempre perdonado," he says respectfully, then stands tall once more.

Korin smiles lightly.

Leaning closer to Marcas, I ask, "What's it mean?"

"Always forgiven."

The magnitude of its meaning shoots right to my heart. All Tate has ever wanted is for his father and brother to see him for who he really is. Not what Ardan has made him out to be. And now, to let go of all that resentment and forgive Korin for the endless years of mistreatment and misunderstandings in one simple yet profound declaration is astounding; truly awe-inspiring.

"Trust takes time, I know. But you'll soon see I'm on your side. Always have been." Tate smiles encouragingly. It looks so foreign to me that I need to remind myself that he's one of the good guys.

Korin extends his arm, and Tate does likewise. They clasp each other's forearms and shake.

"I won't displace my trust again. For that, I pledge." Korin puts his other hand on Tate's shoulder. "You saved Shae. Saved us all."

Tate smiles proudly, and it makes me happy.

"Hey, you two done yet?" Sam calls. "We need an update, and I need to eat before my insides eat themselves."

"Yes! Thank you," Niall says, heading for the stairs.

Mumbling in agreement, everyone else follows.

"We'll be there in a sec," Marcas says, holding me back.

When the door upstairs opens, Tax comes running down, circles us like a whirlwind while sniffing our legs, howls, and then darts to the center of the yard, still sniffing for danger. He makes a muffled growl, then emits another sharp howl.

Marcas pulls me close. "Did Ardan hurt you? I can't believe I put you in danger *again*! I should have listened to my gut."

"Marcas, I'm fine. Really. Tate came before there was any real danger."

His eyes furrow. A deep vee creases into his forehead. "You are a brave woman, Shae. So very brave."

I try to smile, happy to hear him say such things, but it falls flat when I remember we're not done yet.

"Come on, there's more." Taking his hand, I pull him up the stairs. Tax follows closely behind.

"You're sure about this?" Korin says as we enter the living room.

Tate nods assuredly.

Sam and Finn are seated at the kitchen table. While Sam clutches an oversized burrito in his hand and tears into it with his teeth, Finn leans back in his seat, rapping his fingernails on the table while staring hard at it.

Niall sits in the armchair.

"Sure, about what?" Marcas asks, stopping us next to Tate and Korin in the center of the living room.

Tax winds around all our legs then wipes his face on my pant leg before sitting at my feet, panting. Marcas and I reach down and pet him together.

"Tate believes Ardan's been in league with Conall well before now," Korin relays.

"He admitted Conall contacted him before coming," Tate says. "Who knows how long he's been spying for him? Months? Years, maybe."

Korin's eyes narrow at Tate.

"Hey, just relaying what we know. I get no pleasure from it."

"He's the reason Conall and the others were at the bar the other night," I add.

Niall huffs. "Makes me sick, Ardan using our friendship to get to Shae. Just like old times, huh?"

"Conall knew we'd eventually find the amulet. Why not send in a spy? Smart move!" Sam adds with his mouth full.

"How did I not see it? Sense such treachery?" Korin says, staring out the window into the afternoon light. "I brought danger into your home. Risked Shae's life."

"That's not on you, Korin," Marcas says. "Ardan made his choice. You couldn't have known what he'd do. Not before. Not today."

"Ardan said Jamie was a recent addition to their agreement," Tate relays, glancing over at Finn. "They must have communicated recently."

Finn turns in his seat, hands fisted on the table as though about to pound down on it. A hard look deepens in his glaring eyes.

"Maybe as early as today," I add, though I wish I didn't have to. "Ardan said we have until one o'clock tomorrow to hand me over, or they'll take me by force."

"Wh-What?" Marcas coughs out as a flash of fury streaks through his eyes.

"Like hell they will!" Niall growls.

"I'd like to see them try!" Sam adds.

"They threaten no survivors if it comes to that," Tate says. "We can't stop this, can we?"

"We're not done for yet," Marcas warns.

"Yeah, but we can kiss any strategy we had goodbye," Sam mumbles, now stuffing his face with what appears to be a brownie. "Ardan would've blabbed it for sure."

Finn slams his fist on the table. "Do we have to keep at this?" Then he bursts from his chair. It slams against the wall and topples over. Going about pacing the living room, he mumbles under his breath, "All this talk is pointless."

My heart leaps into my throat as I cling to Marcas. No one else seems to react to Finn, making me feel stupid.

Marcas, watching Finn, squeezes my hand a little tighter. Then he looks the others in the eye one by one, ending with Korin, who nods once in reply.

"Agreed!" everyone barks at once, as though responding to some unspoken military *Hooah!* moment between them.

I look to Marcas for answers, but he only smiles wearily at me.

I feel a barrier between us like a giant, bothersome vortex of space. One brought on by their supernatural abilities. I will be like them someday. Just not yet.

"Great!" Finn grumbles, stopping in the center of the room. His eyes swell with deep anger. "Now, unless anyone has objections, let's figure out how in the hell we get my girlfriend back!"

Marcas stares sternly at Finn, then shifts his sights to the rest of the room. "What did you find at the shop?"

"Ardan's scent was all over the loading dock," Korin says. "Though, I suppose we now know why."

"Do you think she knew it was Ardan?" I ask. My stomach turns at the thought of her being tricked into going with him.

Korin shakes his head. "He wouldn't risk her resisting. And there's an advantage to playing the victim, not an accomplice."

"She must be so scared," I say, fighting back more worry.

Marcas caresses my knuckle with his thumb and gives me a weary smile. His eyes focus on mine as though doing so will hypnotize me into calmness. They are definitely gorgeous to look at, but nowhere near pervasive enough to fix the level of anxiety and dread I now feel.

"We found trails all over, but they crisscrossed with old ones, muddying the scent," Marcas says, looking at the others. "It was almost too difficult to decipher which direction they were going."

"But not impossible," Niall chimes in.

"Lucky for us, Niall's transformation happened when it did. His sense of smell is like nothing I've ever encountered."

"I picked up on the trail just past the dirt road at the park." Niall grins. "They were headed toward Granite's Ghost Town. Now we have to figure out how to get in, get Jamie, and get out without someone spotting us."

"We take them by surprise," Sam says, wiping his hands with a napkin. "Use a diversion and strike when they're distracted!"

"Divide and surround them," Finn argues.

"But we don't know how many of them there are," Korin says. "It would be done with great risk."

"Are you nuts? There's too many of us to sneak in undetected. We might as well walk in and hand ourselves over!" Finn says.

"But it's still better than the alternative," Niall counters.

"We'll have more of a fighting chance if we stick together." Marcas kisses my hand, then releases it, letting it fall to my side as he begins to pace the room with Finn. "I'm thinking more of a covert operation. Maybe send in Korin, Finn, and Sam to get a head count. See how many of them we're dealing with. Then get word to the rest of us. That way, our numbers are small, but Tate, Niall, and I would be right behind, ready to proceed as planned."

"Sounds viable," Korin says with optimism.

"Beats sitting around here," Finn growls.

"Wait a minute," I say, stepping forward. "What about me? Wh-Who do I go with?"

In an upheaval, I hear all at once, "No, it's too dangerous," and "You can't go!", "No, she should go. It's not safe to stay!", "Are you crazy? You want her to get killed?" and so on, to the point I can't tell anymore who's saying what.

The sharp sting of anger rises inside me.

"Geeze, why don't you just tell me how you really feel?" I snap back, which produces more incoherent arguing from the boys.

I look at Marcas for a sign he agrees with me, and I believe I get my answer with his pressed smile.

"All right, enough!" Marcas thunders. The room goes silent.

Confident in what he's about to say, I prepare for my triumph with a significant smile.

"Shae, you're not going, and that's final."

"Wait, what? I thought—"

He shakes his head.

Heat rushes me like I'm standing in front of an open oven. "You can't stop me from going. No way am I watching everyone I love run off without me *again*!"

"Shae, it's too dangerous. There's no way."

My lungs burn, heavy with every aggressive breath. "Marcas, please don't do this. Not again!"

"I can't let you come," he says a bit softer, but his eyes still hold firm with control.

The amulet, resting under my shirt, warms against my skin. It calls to me. I pull it out and hold it high. "What about this? If it makes me a wolf, it means I'm one of you. You have to take me. I'm stronger than you think. I can help. Please!"

Marcas sighs, his eyes narrowing in conflicting thoughts. "I—"

"Shae's right." Sam smiles at me. "She stood up to Conall and held her own. I was angry before, so I didn't notice, but she's strong."

I gawk at him in utter shock. After what I put him through, Sam was the last person I figured would sway my way. But I'm glad he's on my side.

"Marcas, this is madness." Niall rises from the armchair. "You know as well as I do, the battlefield is no place for a—"

"A what?" I glare. "A girl? Is that what you were going to say? I'm a girl, so what? Doesn't mean I can't fight. Teach me. I can take care of myself!"

"I was about to say human, but whatever," Niall mumbles.

I watch Finn shake his head, agreeing with Marcas and Niall, and it makes my insides boil.

"Thanks a lot, Finn," I say sourly. He doesn't bother to hide his eye roll as he looks away.

His reaction would hurt more if not for the rapid inferno raging inside me. Jamie's gone, and I'll be damned if I'm gonna let them force me out of the rescue.

"She's been chosen for a reason," Tate chimes in. "I see in her a strength—conviction most don't have. The amulet's capabilities are endless and could help in ways we don't know. Maybe—"

"I can't bank on maybes," Marcas counters. "Too much is at stake. Shae, I won't risk it!"

"We can teach her stuff—help her protect herself," Sam says.

"I'm safest with all of you. After Ardan, can't you see that?"

"Separating her might be what Conall wants," Tate adds.

"Their argument has merit, Marcas," Korin says, eyeing him. "She should come."

"Besides. Where would she go?" Sam says in a rush. "Who could watch her like we would? I say she stays with us."

Marcas lets out a deep-throated huff. "Yes, Sam, I heard you the first time. But it doesn't matter. She's not going. End of discussion!" Marcas' words, heavy with absolution, silence the room.

The automatic ice maker in the freezer dumps its load, rumbling like bowling balls into a plastic container underneath it.

Will no one stand up to Marcas? Can he not be reasoned with?

Stifling the nagging feeling to forget the whole thing, I take a deep breath. "Marcas, can we talk for a minute?" I say, walking over to him, smiling. Not giving him the chance to refuse, I pull him toward the hall.

"We need to work out details anyway," Korin says as we move past.

Sam grins at me sheepishly, then winks before the kitchen wall blocks him from view.

Tax trails behind us, stopping just outside the door. He tries to enter, but I stop him with my leg. "Not this time, boy." And I close the door with a quick click of the lock. Then I turn and lean my back against it. Marcas, standing by his bed, folds his arms. An expressionless, unreadable look is on his face.

Swallowing my unease, I lick my lips and walk to the bed, then sit down.

"You're not going to change my mind. My decision is final."

"Join me," I say, patting the mattress as an inviting smile brightens my face.

For a moment, he stands unmoved, but then cautiously sits. I take his hand. Its warmth and softness comfort me. There is no anger in me, just determination.

"You know, back before all this happened, before you knew I had this," I say, turning the necklace over in my other hand, "every time you were near me, it would radiate heat. Like it had its own heat source. It was almost uncomfortable to touch sometimes."

"Really?" His tone is softer, and his eyes brighter. "Amazing that you would notice enough to connect the two."

"Not at first, but eventually. It happened when Conall showed up at Duke's too. But I think it was warning me then."

Marcas' jaw tenses.

"Marcas, I'm telling you; it gives me strength. It did before, and it can do it again. I just know it."

"Maybe what you felt was comfort, but—"

"How can you believe it has the power to find me but not any to keep me safe once it has?"

Marcas is silent. Contemplative.

"You said it yourself; its powers exceed your understanding. Then why can't it give me some just by wearing it?"

"But what if all you have is a connection to it? Feeling its power but not actually being given any. How can you ask me to take such a risk?"

Tears of frustration well up in my eyes, but I fight them off. "Look, I know taking me is risky, but if you want me to rule by your side, you have to trust that I know what I'm talking about."

"Trust has nothing to do with this, Shae. You could be taken! Don't you get that? My whole life has been about finding the amulet and keeping its keeper safe. I knew I would marry, but I never expected this." He gestures to the two of us. "My lineage aside, without you, there is no future for me. That's why I won't let you be where *he* can take you from me! Because if he did, it would end me."

Feeling a tweak of pain in my heart, I exhale. "You don't think that's the same for me?" I say with tears in my eyes. "You think you're the only one who could lose something here? I didn't expect you! Didn't know I could feel like this for someone. I'm all in. No doubts. And I can't be left here wondering if you'll even make it back to me. Don't put me through that, please!"

"I'm sorry I made you stay before, but this is different. You're safest as far away from danger as possible."

"That's just it; I'm not. No one is more qualified to protect me than you. Sam sees it. Why can't you?"

"It's not that simple."

"Yes, it is! I trust you."

"How can you?" Marcas growls, his hand clenched tight around mine. "She did and look what happened!"

"Jamie wasn't your—"

"No!" He then lets out a long sigh. "Not her."

Who could he mea—? "Vevina," I recall in a whisper. I don't mean to. It just came out.

Marcas looks at me, tears rippling in his bloodshot eyes.

"Niall told me."

"She trusted me, and I—"

"Marcas—"

"I don't want to talk about it." Sniffing, he shifts his tense body and looks at the closet door.

"Please, let me be here for you!"

"It's not like I haven't relived it every single day since. Talking about it won't do any good. I can't remember anything." He clenches his fist like he wants to punch something. "To wake up and find no trace of her. To know I had let her down—it kills me. And I can't handle losing you too!"

"Truly horrible for you, Marcas. Unimaginable. But I'm not Vevina, and you're not alone this time. Your brothers will be there. Korin and Tate, too."

"I will not—cannot—put you in a position where there's even the slightest chance something could go wrong. We didn't see Ardan. Who else will turn against us? Who?"

I cannot answer him. The fire in his eyes scares me, but I understand it. Ardan did more than just lie to them; he broke their trust and a commitment more binding than friendship. How could a wound such as that ever heal?

"I will not allow you to go, and I will not yield." Though quiet, his words ring with the finiteness only a king could give. In this moment, I do not feel his equal, but that of a small girl forced into submission.

I try to swallow the dry lump forming in my throat. "I don't appreciate you ordering me around."

"I'm sorry you see it that way. You must understand; I'll do whatever it takes to keep you safe, and if that means saving you from yourself, so be it."

Heat rises from me. "Then what good is this?" I say, clutching the necklace. "If it doesn't prove that I'm meant to be by your side, especially when things get tough?"

"Don't use that against me. It has nothing to do with this."

"It has everything to do with it! I'm here because it chose me. Why can't you see what it sees? I . . . I—" Taking in a sharp breath, I feel a piercing pain surge through my chest and down my arms and legs. I gasp for breath, but none enters my lungs.

"Shae! Are you—what's happening?" Marcas grabs me, his voice distant, as though I'm dreaming. He shakes me, but I do not move.

Inside, I am screaming, fighting with everything I have in me to break free from the agony of being burned alive by fiery pain, scorching like hot liquid metal as it travels through every nerve in my body.

Moments feel like a lifetime. I don't know how much more I can bear.

Desperate to help, Marcas grips my arm, panic in his eyes. "Shae, please!" His hands shake as they draw me to him.

A coolness shifts inside me. Like the spark of a fresh bitten piece of mint gum, the chill moves outward from my chest. My leg twitches. Then my foot and my toes move. My fingers begin to tingle.

"Mar-Marcas. . ."

"Shae!" Marcas grabs my face in his hands. "Are you all right?"

"I think. . ." I say breathlessly. Pain continues to dissipate until only the memory of it remains.

"What happened?"

"It was like fire, everywhere." Feeling weak, I dab sweat from my brow and try to steady my breathing.

Marcas' eyebrows crease. "Impossible."

"What?"

"But how can that be?"

Grabbing his arm, I shake it. "Marcas?"

When he looks at me, bewilderment lifts from his eyes, and he smiles. "How do you feel now? The pain all gone?"

I nod. "Better, yeah." Extending my arm down, I twist and flex. "Ouch! That hurts."

"Tight, here?" He gently squeezes my tricep.

"Ow, yes!" I shake my arm.

Marcas beams at me as if proud of something I've done. "I can't believe . . . It shouldn't be possible, Shae, but I think you've transitioned."

"I have?"

"Well, not completely. Come on." He supports me as he pulls me up and we head for the door. Laying on the floor outside it, Tax scurries to the side when it opens, and then he follows us into the living room.

"Listen up." Marcas stops us in the center of the room. All eyes focus on him. "Plans have changed. Shae's coming with us, but she needs a crash course in combat. Any takers?"

While everyone else's mouth drops, Sam's hand shoots up, a look of eager excitement flashing in his eyes.

CHAPTER 3

Hour Of Reckoning

Hoping to land a solid hit, I jab my right fist with all my might at Sam's right side. With a hefty thwack, I make direct contact. He grunts, and I smile wide.

"Nice." He grimaces, rubbing his shoulder.

"Getting better." My grin broadens.

"Indeed!" Sam shifts his weight, pivots, and whirls around, whacking me in the back of the head like it was nothing. "But don't get cocky." He winks. "Anticipate the counterattack, or you could find yourself in a bad situation."

Cringing while rubbing my head, I fling hair from out of my face, and breathlessly say, "Got it," as I wipe sweat from my brow.

"Have it down? Or do you wanna go again?" He does a little bounce and a hoppity-hop on the tips of his toes sort of dance.

"Next." I breathe out.

"All right." He grins, impressed. "Let's work on the sneak attack. You put your legs like this," he says, spreading my feet wide. "Hands here." He shifts my fisted hands and arms up front. "But keep your face forward, eyes looking as wide around the side of your head as possible. Good, now can you see Korin?"

"I-I think—yes, he's by the deck."

"Awesome. Now what about Marcas?"

"By the log!"

"Good, okay, so now what I want you to do if someone comes at you from either side—behind even, if you're quick enough—is crouch, grab their leg and arm, and hurl!" He grunts as he plays out the scenario. "Got it?"

I give him a thumbs up.

"Ready to give it a try?"

I nod, correct my stance, and raise my arms.

Niall suddenly comes at me with a punch from the left. I block it with my forearm. A second later, Korin kicks at me from the right which I deflect with my other arm. Then I steady my stance, ready for Sam.

But he does not come. With my eyes forward, I stretch my vision as far to the sides as I can. Still no Sam.

"Ahhhh!" Sam yells from behind.

Instinctively, I pivot, crouch, grab his leg and arm, hurl him up and over my back, and toss him onto his back on the other side of me.

Korin and Niall burst into roaring laughter while Sam groans, "Nicely done," as he rolls onto his side, holding his ribs.

"You good?" I ask, bending over him and reaching out my hand for him to take. He scowls and shushes my hand away, causing Niall to sputter and laugh. I shrug, then walk away.

Marcas, still on the log with Tax by his side, smiles at me, though he does not move to join me under the deck while I drink water.

"Phew, you got some moves," Tate says, standing up. "Remind me never to piss you off." He grins.

"Want to go a round?" I say and nudge his arm, giving a playful smirk.

"What a fantastic idea," Sam says as he walks up to us, seemingly all better.

"Uh, yeah . . . no." Tate shakes his head rigidly. "I'm good."

"You know, for not having fully transitioned into a wolf, your size and mediocre body mass sure do pack a killer wallop." Sam chuckles. "Wonder how far you throw." Sam eyes Tate with a grin.

"Nope!" Tate steps away. "Not gonna happen."

"Dude, she needs the practice," Sam adds seriously, though his eyes gleam.

"I, for one, am very interested to see how strong she's gotten," Korin says as he walks up to us. "I mean, it's only fair, brother, that you lend your skills in this matter. For Shae's benefit, of course." Korin smirks as he turns to look at me.

"Come on," Sam taunts. "Just do it."

Tate huffs and rolls his eyes. "Fine, but no throwing."

Sam claps loudly once. "All right, let's do this!"

Tate and I trek to the center of the yard and prepare to battle.

"Like wrestling," Niall says as he stands between us. "First person to get the other over their line wins. Ready. Set. Go!"

Tate and I move in a circle around each other. He thrusts forward to get me, but I shift to the side. I counter with a jab to his ribcage, but he dodges to the right.

"Boring. Come on, shove him!" Niall chants.

I give Tate a raised eyebrow, to which he shrugs back. Then we move in on each other. With a swift step to the left, then right, I am to him in a flash. I shove him with what feels like a normal amount of force, but the motion sends him flying well past the line Niall said was out. He skids to a stop on his back, halfway across the yard.

Under the deck, Korin subtly chuckles while Sam leans against a post, laughing hysterically.

"Noice!" Niall calls, running to me. "Dang, that boy flew!" Then he laughs some more.

"One more go at it, Tate!" Sam hollers, then laughs.

Standing up, Tate brushes himself off. Dark, blackish muck is caked on his back and left side.

Cringing, I ask, "Tate, you all right?" while I walk to him.

"Don't I look it?" he mumbles, stretching around to see his backside. Then he sighs.

"I'm really sorry, Tate; I didn't mean—"

"Whatever, it's fine. You needed the practice, right?" He huffs, then shrugs. When he looks at me again, I can't stop a small smile from appearing. For a flickering moment, I see a smirk on his pressed lips, but then it's gone.

"Sorry," I say again as he walks past, moving towards the house and the noisy boys giving him a hard time.

"Guys, stop," I say, walking up to them. "Leave him be."

"We about ready?" Marcas asks as he and Tax walk up to Sam, who's guzzling water in loud gulps.

"Yeah," he replies, panting for air. "She's got strength, man. Bet she could even throw you!"

Marcas half smiles, then turns to me. "You feel ready?"

I nod assuredly. "Did you see me?"

He gives a small smile.

"Just hope I don't freeze."

"You'll do fine."

"I better get cleaned up," I say, then head up the stairs.

The front door is ajar, so I step in slowly. The house is quiet, as if empty, but I know Finn is inside somewhere. I walk down the hall and into the kitchen and see him sitting on the small couch by the window. Looking out it, he sighs.

Not wanting to bother him, I slowly turn around.

"You did good . . . out there," he says quietly.

Giving pause, I then turn back to him, my lips pressed. I want to say how sorry I am for Jamie, but I think better of it.

"She's all right. I know she is." He turns to look at me, the worry in his eyes running as deep as my own.

"If anyone can get through this, it's Jamie. She's tough, Finn." I'm not sure if I'm trying to convince myself or him, but the need to believe it grips me.

He nods.

"I'm sorry we've taken so much time, I—"

"Don't. Shae, if it were Jamie, I'd want her ready. You needed time for this."

First, I give him a small, warm smile. Then I exhale, releasing the guilt I've been holding on to since Marcas called for my training.

Leaving Finn to his thoughts, I return to Marcas' bedroom. Several minutes later, I hear people talking loudly in the hall.

A soft, triple knock sounds at the door. "Shae, you ready?" Marcas call.

"Almost. Be out in a sec," I reply as I pull my shirt over my head and check myself in the mirror. Looking closer, I examine my face, then my arms, to see if my physical features have changed at all, like Niall's had. I find everything to be as it was before. No one will know I've transitioned. An advantage I hope to keep hidden for as long as possible.

Grabbing a jacket before I head out, I then follow the rumblings of voices toward the front of the house. Marcas and Sam are by Finn, still sitting on the small couch. Niall and Tate are at the table. I move to the corner between the two couches and sit on one of the arms. Tax trots up to me and puts his wet nose on my knee. A whimper sort of huff shakes his body.

"Sorry, Tax, you'll have to stay." His pouty eyes shift as he blinks. "Don't look at me like that."

Dropping a bag of supplies on the ground in the hall, Korin says, "Everything's ready." Then he moves to stand by Marcas.

"You know what to do, Sam?" Marcas asks.

"Yeah, they should be distracted. Eating dinner, hopefully. We'll get into position, then wait. Conall will show soon enough."

"And those with him," Korin affirms.

Niall punches his fist into his palm. "Let's do this."

"Let's go." Finn stands. His narrow, cold eyes glare at the hallway, his jaw clenched.

I wouldn't trade places with that fool, Ardan, for anything. Finn has enough pent-up anger to do the unthinkable, though I hope he doesn't.

Niall and Tate move to the center of the room, joining the others. I remain where I am.

"A ten-minute head start should be enough. Stick to the plan, no matter what." Marcas eyes Sam, who, for once, nods instead of saying something snarky.

Marcas then looks at me. His eyes are warm, yet I see the weight of our plan, the outcome, and our uncertain future flickering in their reflection.

I swallow hard, realizing that before, when I thought of this moment, it seemed so far away. Now, it feels like time has fast-forwarded, bringing me face-to-face with it. Hesitation is thick on my tongue, but I smile it away as I stand up and go to Marcas.

"You're with me, Mo Chroi," he says, wrapping his arm around my shoulder as we follow everyone down the hall and out the door. "Niall and Tate, too. We'll hold back and wait for the go-ahead."

While we move single file down the stairs, my insides flop with an upheaval of uncertainty and dread.

Finn, Sam, and Korin take off running into the forest the second they reach the ground. Marcas opens the passenger-side door of my car. He closes it after I get in. Tate and Niall sit in the back.

As Marcas puts the car in reverse and backs down the driveway, he glances at me. "We'll drive about half a mile from their hideout and wait." Then he shifts the car into drive, and we go forward.

"Which road are you taking?" I ask.

"The main one's too obvious. They'd know we were coming from a mile away," Niall says, staring out his side window at the scenery. Or maybe he's double-checking for our enemy. It could be either, I suppose.

"There's a clearing a half a mile below the town that will take you there too," I say.

Marcas smiles. "We're headed there now. Here." He lightly tosses a dark, cobalt blue vile of liquid at me.

"What's this?" I say, examining it closer. The thick liquid moves like oil, slowly traveling along the side as

I turn the vile upside down then upright again. Twisting the dropper lid off, I take a sniff. "Wow, that's strong." I cough and cover my nose. "Kind of stinks." The content smells strongly of earth and pine, with hints of juniper, sagebrush and a bitter berry I can't place. But the light fragrance of roses lingering after the others dissipate is surprising.

"Essense of stink," Niall snickers.

"It's supposed to. How else is it going to hide your scent?" Tate says.

"Marcas had us sneaking it on you whenever we were around you," Niall adds.

"Seriously?" Subtly, I sniff myself, wondering how bad I stink.

"Don't worry, usually you smell like spicy Gardinas and coconut." Marcas winks.

My cheeks rush red. "Well, you smell like sandalwood and pine, so . . ."

"I do?" He smiles. "Interesting. Well, regardless of how bad it smells, it kept Conall from tracking you after that day in the woods."

"Really?" I say astounded, though I refrain from admitting that I hadn't given the logistics of what had happened much thought. Now that I have, it seems near impossible for me to have remained unnoticed for so long without help. Conall, himself, even admitted his frustration in my ability to elude him. "Pt-h, and here I thought you were being sweet on me, trying to see me as much as you could. Nope, just stinkin' me up with this!" I snicker.

"Both, actually." Marcas' smile widens. "But unfortunately, that stuff also masks you from us, so we had to stay close to keep you safe. But not too close."

"Hah, you call showing up everywhere I was, not close?" I smirk.

"Pshaw," Niall snorts. "You know you loved hangin' with us all that time!"

"Sure, I did." I tease back. "So how does it work? Why can't I smell it on me?"

"Korin developed a baseline serum that we then add smells from the area we're trying to remain undetected. In this case Beargrass, some flowers and dirt—pine. All things you've probably smelled thousands of times, but you're so used to them you didn't notice. You better put some on," Marcas says, nudging his head toward the bottle. "We'll be there in a minute."

When I open the bottle again, the smell smacks me in the face. But when I smell my wrist after applying a little dab to it, I smell nothing, like Marcas said. "Hmm no smell."

"Wow, are you kidding?" Niall coughs. "It burns my throat." He motions for me to pass him the vile while holding his breath, then he blots some on his neck before handing it to Tate.

"It will until applied. No smell means it's working," Tate says, dotting some behind his ear, then he hands it back to Marcas.

A minute later, we turn down the road I had mentioned before, and then drive for about five more minutes before parking. Getting out of the car, we then travel on foot down a long, bumpy path scarcely visible through the overgrowth.

"This is it. Korin and the others should be up there." Marcas points just ahead. "On the other side of that hill."

I suddenly feel so impressed by him. He's so brave and put-together. So much a leader.

"I love you, you know," I say to him, not caring if the others hear me.

Marcas kisses me. "I'm counting on it." Then he grins, flashing his adorable dimples at me.

A few feet away from us, Tate and Niall punch at the air, high kneeing it in place, preparing their bodies for battle.

"Wait, you're not changing?" I ask.

"Can't." Niall grunts, stretching his legs.

"The town's gone, but the boundaries remain. We won't know what we're dealing with until we get up there," Marcas says.

"Oh. . ."

"You seem disappointed."

"No." I force a small smile. "I just kind of imagined it would be like last time. All wolves except me."

"I will not be changing," Marcas affirms.

I want to ask why not, but the finiteness in his tone tells me the reason doesn't matter. He will do what he thinks is best, regardless of one's opinion of it.

"One more thing. Try to be as quiet as possible. With the wind and who knows how many men up there making noise, we will most likely go unheard, but we don't want to risk it."

I nod and wonder if my labored breathing will be enough to give me away.

For a moment, we are silent. The stillness brings with it a sense of anticipation. A battle is coming, even though the tranquility of the forest tries to make us forget. People will get hurt. Or worse. The thought makes my stomach turn and my heart pound so hard that I can feel the vibrations through my body.

"Look!" Niall whispers, pointing up the hill. "By the broken tree. Sam's waving."

"Time to go," Tate says, walking past us.

I hold my breath expectantly.

"Stay close." Marcas kisses me, then grabs my hand as we make our way up the hill.

CHAPTER 4

Underestimated

The gusty wind brushes against the leaves in the thick forest around us. It grows eerily louder the closer we get to the top of the hill.

Sam is waiting at the base of a portly pine tree. Its full-needled branches keep him hidden. Finn and Korin are crouched low to his right, peeking through a wide hedge that seems to travel on for several feet past them. Though thick, they are still thin enough in spots to see through.

"How many?" Marcas asks as he squats down between Sam and Finn. The rest of us do likewise.

Knowing they use telepathy, I am thankful they are keen enough to clue me vocally to what's going on.

"Five, so far. Conall went in there." Korin points to an old, dilapidated building on the right, about thirty yards away. The windows are void of glass, the front door is missing, and the porch is a good two feet or more off the ground. The steps seem to have crumbled years ago.

"He had four guards with him, and someone cloaked in black. I didn't get a good look, though," Sam whispers.

"Keep an eye out for more. What about Tavis or Rogan? Ardan? Any sign of them?" Marcas asks.

Finn shifts in his squat. "Guarding Jamie, I bet."

"We could—" Tate suddenly flinches, Finn having gripped his shirt firmly.

"Shhh," Finn hisses silently with his finger to his lips, then points to a patch of trees with a trail winding out across from the big building. Several burly men appear, with Tavis at the front. A ridiculously stupid, smug smile rests on his chiseled face. Rogan, with his large, gruesome facial scar, appears, dragging Jamie and Ardan along. Finn takes in a sharp breath but, surprisingly, stays still, while my heart leaps spastically in my chest.

Rogan then forces the prisoners over to the building. They wait outside while he hoists himself through the open door and disappears.

Jamie takes a subtle step away from the guard. Then another. He looks up and tugs her back. She glares loathingly at him and huffs.

"That's Luc?" I mouth, pointing to the lanky kid on the other side of Jamie.

Marcas nods.

I mime, "What the hell does Ardan think he is doing?" as I point to his bound hands like Jamie's.

"Deceiving," Marcas mouths back.

"He's good at that," Niall whispers.

Wordlessly, Finn and Sam shush him, their eyes blazing.

Rogan returns to the doorway of the building, where he inspects his surroundings before jumping down. When his feet hit the ground, dust billows up and drifts across the ground. He then stands to the side with his arms folded like always.

A minute later, Conall appears and leaps down, followed by a tall, slender figure in a hooded robe, just like Sam had described. They jump from the building with smooth, effortless movements, as though suspended by invisible wires, gently lowering them to the ground.

Finn's entire body tenses. Reaching out, Marcas places a hand on his shoulder. Without breaking focus on Conall, Finn nods once.

Tavis peers around while conversing briefly in hushed tones with Conall. After a moment, they both turn their backs on us.

Unknowingly, I have been gripping Marcas' arm so tight that my knuckles have turned white and now tingle. I shake the numbness away before resuming my grip on him.

"You can stop manhandling me now!" Jamie says, jerking her arm away from her nameless captor. He grunts and seizes her arm again.

"Jamie, what an honor to have you join us," Conall says coolly.

"Honor is all yours," Jamie counters with a sneer.

Good old Jamie. Never the victim, even when she is presumed to be one.

"Get these creeps to keep their hands off me!"

"A necessary evil, my dear. We can't have you try to run away again."

"You can't keep me here!"

With a quick flick, the cloaked stranger at Conall's side swings their hand, smacking Jamie in the cheek. When Jamie winces away, the person then leans in and mutters something my meager ears can't hear, though Finn hammers his fists into the ground, his hostility visible in every strained vein in his neck and arms. Sam puts a hand on his arm, which Finn grudgingly flings off.

"Please refrain from roughing up the captives," Conall says calmly, though I see a glimmer of irritation in his eye. "Could fuel our enemy's need for vengeance."

They bow their head dutifully.

"Conall, enough!" Ardan growls from behind Jamie. Rogan moves from his post and shoves Ardan past Jamie to face Conall, then goes back to his station.

"You're absolutely right, Ardan. It's quite time we ended this game of charades," Conall slaps Ardan on the back while one of the men unties his wrists. "You've made your choice, though I don't see the appeal. But I guess with a little effort, you could whip her sharp tongue into submission. Don't envy you though, but best of luck."

Jamie's eyes widen.

A sly smile encompasses Tavis' face. "Now, isn't that a sight? The bitty's speechless." Then he laughs robustly, as do a few of the other men standing around. Ardan smiles too, but more likely out of genuine excitement for Jamie being there with him than for the mockery at her expense.

Finn shifts his weight on his toes, his fists clutching tufts of grass. His teeth are clenched so tightly that they could shatter under the pressure.

I understand his rage, because I feel it too—an overwhelming urge to punch that guy square in the face. But, like Finn, I must dig deep to find restraint to avoid drawing attention.

Tavis smirks at Jamie with obvious disdain. "Don't tell me you believed Ardan's horrible rescue attempt. Rogan could do a better job with his eyes closed." He snorts, then turns and walks the curved path to the right of the old building, falling out of sight.

"You incredible jackass! You brought me here, didn't you? You . . . You traitor!"

Ardan smiles coolly as he removes the rope binding her.

"I'll leave you to it." Conall motions with his hand for the mystery person to follow him. "Luc. You three." He points to the men behind Ardan and Jamie. "Keep watch."

Ardan bows respectfully to Conall, then watches him walk away before laying eyes on Jamie again. She is staring hard at him with narrowed eyes, full of blood-red fury.

He chuckles lightheartedly. "Trust me. Everything will be all right."

"Why would I *ever* trust a backstabbing creep like you? I can't believe you did this!"

"Hey, nothing's changed other than what side we're on."

"Excuse me? What side *you're* on! I'm not a part of this!"

"And yet, would it be so bad if you were? We'd have everything we've ever wanted. Just you and me."

"Not in this lifetime, Buddy!"

"I hope you're not waiting for Finn to come save you. Because he won't. He told me himself that you're just a fling. A passing fun time. I doubt he even cares you're missing."

"Liar!"

"Look around, Sweetheart. Do you see anyone coming for you? I don't. It's been hours. If they were, they'd be here by now. Face it, Shae's who they really care about. And she's too spineless and selfish to risk her own life to save yours. To the others, you're just a tag-along friend. An afterthought. Of no importance in the grand scheme of things."

My heart breaks for her. If she only knew—we're right here!

Jamie growls and shoves him. "That's not true! You did something to them!"

Ardan pushes Jamie to the side. She stumbles and falls at Luc's feet. He reaches down to help, but Ardan glares at him, so he straightens up and stares forward.

Finn lurches, ready to dart across the field, but Marcas pulls him back before our cover is blown.

Without looking, Marcas takes my hand and squeezes it. I know he can sense the tumultuous screams of protest swirling inside my mind.

Ardan steps forward. "I have no reason to hurt them. My deal is for you. I care about you. You must know that by now." He stretches out a helping hand to Jamie.

Looking up at him, she scowls and hits it away, then gets up on her own.

"Conall's a decent guy once you get to know him," Ardan continues with a cheerful, somewhat excited tone. "If you stay, we'll be provided for—treated like royalty."

Finn huffs, watching Ardan like a lion and its prey.

"And, what? Am I supposed to just forget that you condemned my best friend to a life of misery with that jerk?"

The smile on Ardan's lips flattens. "I'll do what I must if it keeps you here."

"*Come on*—do you even hear yourself? Marcas will never hand Shae over! Nothing will keep them apart. Not me! Not you! Not some lunatic trying to force her into marriage! Nothing!"

"And yet." Ardan's eyes narrow. "Sometimes even the ones closest to us can still surprise us. Especially when the right leverage is used."

"Not Marcas. Never! But I guess turning your back on friends—on family—comes easily for a selfish jerk like you!" Jamie jabs Ardan's shoulder. He raises his hand to strike her but stops in midair. She winces away.

Marcas quickly releases my hand and forces Finn to sit back down yet again, using both hands this time. I wonder how much more Finn will put up with before he turns around and decks Marcas.

Ardan stares Jamie down, his eyes flaming with anger. "You'll have to learn to bite that bitter tongue of yours if you wish to survive this. I'm willing to give us a go if you are. Otherwise, I'll need to reevaluate my prospects. Conall has little tolerance for petulance. I fear you wear his patience thin."

"I don't care! It's pathetic; to agree to rip apart two people who love each other just so you can play King of the Mountain, or forest, or whatever! And you're dead wrong if you think for a minute that you can keep me from the man I love. I swear, I'll make your life a living hell as long as I'm breathing."

"Enough, Woman! I spared you once, but don't test my willpower." Grabbing her by the arm, he sneers. "I get it; you'd rather die. And if you're not careful, that can easily be arranged.

I hoped you'd listen to reason, because if you're not with me, you're with no one. Perhaps you should weigh your options before dismissing life with me so hastily." Ardan breathes out deeply, his nostrils flaring. But when he speaks again, his tone is neutral, though he grips her arm. "Of course, ultimately, it's up to you, but I hope, for your sake, you choose me. I'd hate to see something bad happen to you."

Ardan then thrusts Jamie at Luc. "Take her back, lock her up tight, and make sure Rogan sees to her evening meal. We can't have the lovely starve."

With a pivot of his feet, Ardan turns and leaves the same way the others had gone, having two of the three men follow him.

While Jamie rubs her arm where Ardan's death grip had been, Luc ties her wrists. Leaning in, they converse too quietly for anyone else to hear.

"Move on," the other guard says, shoving Jamie forward. Luc hurries to her side and stays there as they walk.

"Wait," Marcas whispers as Finn and Sam begin to rise. They crouch back down in a huff.

"Oy, faster!" The guard growls again and shoves Jamie harder. She stumbles and falls to the ground.

"Hey! You heard Conall; don't hurt the prisoner," Luc says, pushing the guard back. Then he puts out a hand for Jamie to take. She flicks it aside.

"Make you feel big and tough," Jamie grunts, struggling to get up with her hands tied together, "pushing helpless women around?"

This time, when Luc grasps her elbow, she lets him help.

"Don't have the guts to do it when my hands aren't tied, huh?" She scowls at the guard.

"Quiet, woman!" He comes at Jamie, but Luc blocks him.

"Bodin, head back to camp!"

With eyes narrowed into slits, Bodin snarls at Luc as if he's about to hit him. Then he thrusts his upper body hard into Luc's, forcing him to stumble back.

"That's an order!" Luc breathes out, stepping up on him again.

Bodin grunts and knocks Luc aside, then walks toward the buildings.

Luc and Jamie continue down the path to the left, soon shifting out of sight.

"I think I know where he's headed," Marcas says, gathering everyone in.

"Not if we stop him first!" Finn says as though he'd been reading Marcas' mind.

"If we hurry, we can cut them off before they head back over the town's limits.

Finn. Sam. Go further out, around the field to the other side and come in on their right. Korin, you and Niall stay to the left. At the halfway point, turn and wait in case they veer off in another direction."

Korin nods.

"Shae, you and I will corral them in while Tate takes the rear. Let's move," Marcas says in a rush as he leads me in the same direction Luc had just taken Jamie.

"Be safe," Tate says as we hurry by.

"Watch yourself," I warn back.

And then we run. The trees flash by us like a big, green blur. The adrenaline pumping through my body fuels me forward at a pace I am not accustomed to. My lungs start to burn as I gasp for breath. Reaching the point of collapsing, I slow down.

Marcas follows in stride. "They should be passing by Niall and Korin any minute now," he says, breathing like he'd been standing still. I, on the other hand, wheeze like an asthmatic, bent over with my hands on my knees, ready to vomit at any moment.

Several feet away from us, I hear talking coming through the trees. Marcas points toward the sound and then motions where I should follow him. He grabs my hand, and we are on the move again. My eyes stay on the ground, watching for twigs and branches. Using fluent, intentional movements, Marcas maneuvers us through the gauntlet of trees. When the forest edge draws near, we stop. Just beyond is a spacious field. The trail Jamie travels on runs down the center of it toward us.

Watching from behind a large tree across from Marcas, I see Tate slyly following Jamie and Luc some distance behind them. It is a wonder they do not see him. Though I know due to the serum, his scent is camouflaged.

They draw nearer. My heart thumps wildly. My sweaty hands, clenched in fists, tremble. I bring them to my chest as I take a deep breath and hold it in.

Any moment now.

Marcas counts down on his fingers. When he hits one, we jump out just as Jamie and Luc reach the trees. At the same time, Korin and the others burst from their seclusion, creating a circle around them.

Jamie and Luc skid to a halt.

"Marcas? Wh-what are you doing here?" she gasps. "Shae? You shouldn't be here!"

Before Luc has time to stop him, Korin clutches Luc's biceps and yanks back.

"Jamie!" I call, pulling her away.

With tears in her eyes, Jamie hugs me so tight that I can scarcely breathe. Her body trembles in my arms.

"Stop resisting!" Korin tightens his grip on Luc.

"Lemme go!" Luc tugs back, then tries to turn around and kick Korin in the leg.

"Try that again, and I'll block you up the side of the head!"

Luc then spits at him and tries to headbutt him, so Korin makes good on his threat, causing Luc to cry out in pain.

Marcas steps forward. "Enough, Luc. We don't want trouble. Just Jamie."

Luc stops struggling and scowls at Marcas. "I wasn't gonna hurt her, I—"

"Oh, no, just out for a stroll, are you?" Finn says angrily, stepping up on Luc. But Marcas puts his hand out, stopping him from getting too close. Luc lowers his gaze, appearing unwilling to look Finn in the eyes.

"Marcas, no!" Jamie gasps and pulls away from me. "He's not with Conall! He's helping me." Pools of tears rest under her eyes. She wipes them away as she runs to Luc.

"Jamie, I can handle this. Just-just get back," Luc says through clenched teeth. But she does not leave.

"Go against his brother? No chance!" Sam says with disgust.

Finn, like a puppy in a window, stares at Jamie, but she does not take her eyes off Marcas, who's watching Luc contemplatively.

"Marcas, we can't believe *him*! He's Conall's brother!" Korin says, tugging Luc close. "Rather convenient, don't you think? Choosing now to go against Conall. The whole thing stinks like a trap."

Luc winces. "Believe what you want, but it's true. I can't—I can't take the constant berating anymore. His ridicule. Making these girls pawns in his scheme.

71

It's sick! I won't be forced to be a part of it anymore. I won't!"

"Marcas, please! He isn't like the rest of them! He can't change who his brothers are. Let him go. Please!"

"I never wanted to help him. He made me. I had no choice. But I'm done. With or without your help, I'm gone! Never coming back."

Giving pause, Marcas looks at me. Through his eyes, he begs me to decide for him what to do.

"It's your call. But I trust Jamie."

Marcas turns to Korin and gives him a single nod. Korin opens his mouth to protest, but Marcas' firm eye stops him. Korin takes a second before begrudgingly letting Luc go.

Luc rubs his tender arms, eyeballing Korin. Then he takes a cautionary step away from everyone.

Jamie runs and jumps into Finn's outstretched arms. As she wraps her arms around his neck, he kisses her as though he can't get enough.

"I've got you . . . my love," he whispers between kisses.

"Ardan said . . . you wouldn't . . . come for me," she says breathlessly through his kisses.

Finn holds her face close to his. Anger and concern shift in his eyes. "I could never leave you. *Ever*," he says in a stern whisper, which makes her cry profusely.

"I kn-I knew he was lying!"

Finn pulls Jamie close, muffling the sounds of her sobs in the process. Slowly, he then holds out a hand to Luc. "Thank you for protecting Jamie."

Luc hesitates, then accepts Finn's offer. "It wasn't fair that she got involved in the first place." Then he looks at Jamie.

She smiles back at him through her tears and then looks at Marcas. "He can't stay here! If Conall found out—"

"Agreed," Marcas says while grabbing my hand. "Which is why it's time to go."

"This way!" Jamie points the way she and Luc had been headed before. "There's a car just down there."

"We should hurry. They'll be on to us soon enough," Luc says, moving.

Rumbling toward us like the steady beats of pounding drums comes the robust roar of a familiar, malicious laugh. The haunting, echoey sound turns the blood in my veins to ice.

CHAPTER 5

Where Battles Lie

"Be ready!" Marcas pulls me close. I tug Jamie with me. The others shift themselves widely around us.

A gust of wind pounds against the trees like a whirlwind of dread temporarily drowning out the thumping of my heartbeat in my ears.

Jamie grips my arm, her gaze flitting around. Taking a hold of the amulet, I breathe out. Its growing warmth encourages me to be brave.

"My dear brother, we were never unaware of your hasty retreat," Conall calls from the shadows in a break in the trees at the other end of the field. Men and wolves follow him as he steps forward. "Quite expected it, actually."

Marcas grabs my arm, making me gasp as at least fifty of Conall's warriors, both men and wolves, scramble from the trees.

"Naturally, Luc, it wasn't a huge stretch of the imagination to think you would betray us the first chance you got." Conall chuckles sardonically as he comes toward us. "In fact, we were counting on it. Why else would we entrust our valuable prisoner with such a pathetic specimen like yourself?"

"It's over!" Luc hollers. "I don't have to listen to you anymore."

"How unfortunate. You think they'll live long enough to get you free." Conall blurts out a condescending laugh, then abruptly stops. His face turns to stone. "But seeing how you prefer them over us, I'll be sure to let you die alongside them. My parting gift to you."

Luc's face pales as his body wobbles, his legs unsteady underneath him.

"I just love it when things work out, don't you, Marcas? Now, if you don't mind, allow one of my men to remove Shae from harm's way so we can get on with it."

Marcas brings me closer while Korin and Tate station themselves behind us. Niall and Sam then close in the circle. Finn stays with Jamie by my side, as does Luc. He looks at me and nods before facing the oncoming men.

From the thick of the forest come the cries of protest. "Wait! Conall, you're mistaken. All but one must die!" Ardan yells in a panic as he runs from the trees into the field. Struggling to get through the hordes of soldiers who refuse to move, Ardan huffs. "You promised . . . Jamie to me. We-We had a deal!"

"And plans change." Conall stares at Ardan and gives a sly smirk as if it brings him immense joy to double-cross. "You're welcome to reverse paths if you prefer—join your sweetheart before her demise."

Ardan stops. As the crowd advances, he is engulfed, disappearing until only the memory of his cowardly expression remains.

Conall then turns his attention back to us and continues his advance. "Now, the girl, please."

Marcas' eyes narrow, yet his lips are lax as if a secret rests behind them. "Not today. Shae made her choice," he says coolly with a mocking smile. "You remember, right? You were there."

Even with the distance between us, I can still see Conall's fiery, hot eyes brighten with anger as his jaw grits tight.

"As if it matters! She'll learn to live with our arrangement or be put down. It makes no difference to me," he says, as though the memory of his horrifying, grief-stricken howls could be silenced with professedly hollow words. And yet their finiteness still causes prickling chills to run rampant down my spine. "Now, step aside!"

"No!" Marcas says, his deep tone resonating with the authoritative power of a mighty king.

Conall's men shift aside just enough to let the enigmatic hooded figure—who has seemingly materialized out of thin air—move forward.

"Ah, yes, right on time," Conall muses with satisfaction. "No sudden movements, now. We wouldn't want Shae to get hurt."

Slow and steady, the figure glides toward us and comes to a stop in front of Marcas. A large gray wolf is at their side. It snarls its snout at me, baring spiky, red-stained teeth.

Marcas shifts me behind his back and raises his fists, ready to strike anyone stupid enough to come for me.

"Finn, don't leave Jamie's side; you hear me?" I whisper sharply. "I don't care what happens next; you keep her safe! Jamie, I mean it—go, no matter what!"

Jamie, who's been gripping my hand since the moment Conall showed himself, nods and lets me go, then clings to Finn's arm. Finn affirms to me the plan with a nod of his own.

The figure gestures to two men to take me. Stepping forward, one of them stretches out his hand as if Marcas will willingly let me go, but Marcas tugs him forward and whips him around, flinging him away, then shoves another man trying to get me.

Three more men come at us. Two try to seize Marcas at the same time. They succeed for about a half-second before Marcas slams their heads together, knocking them unconscious in a heap at our feet. Marcas kicks them away with his feet, then steadies himself with a *'you sure you want to try that too'* look in his eyes as he waits for the third warrior to make his move.

"I can do this all day," Marcas smirks. The warrior falters, then steps back.

"You and what army?" Conall's men step to the side and bow as he walks through. When he stops in front of Marcas, the hooded figure shifts so they are on Conall's right. "Surrender with dignity. Don't let your brothers die for a lost cause."

"I warned you, Conall. You can try, but you will never win!" Marcas stands up tall, towering over everyone around us as a dominating sort of scowl hardens his features.

"You should yield while you still can," Conall says with an evil grin. "There's no need to make Shae witness your mangled, lifeless body."

Marcas huffs. "I'll take my chances."

"Look!" one of Conall's men yells, pointing to some trees.

"There!" another one hollers, pointing in the opposite direction.

A muffled rumble travels through the forest from just beyond the exterior of the open field. With the roaring sound of a million warriors, sixty-plus towering men with gigantic wolves flanking them sprint into the clearing from all directions. They bombard Conall's men with bounding fury.

"Go! Now!" I yell and shove Finn. He grabs Jamie and leads her to the safety of the trees.

A handful of Conall's men yell and charge at us, each targeting a member of my circle. Two of them advance on Marcas. He manages to land several punches before breaking free, only to be assaulted by more of them.

"Protect Shae!" Marcas yells while picking up one of the men and hurls him into a bunch of their cohorts advancing.

Sam sprints to Marcas and starts punching every guy who comes near, while Niall, Tate, and Korin step in closer to me, keeping the barrier around me in tight formation. With their feet planted firmly in place, they keep shoving men and wolves back like mob security at a rock concert. It gives the others a perfect target to land kicks and punches on as they drive them back.

Conall tries to shove his way through the hordes of persistent attackers to get to me, but they keep blocking his way. He expels a monstrous growl and thrashes around to dislodge himself from the mob of fighting men now towing him away, like the powerful riptide of a roaring ocean.

A massive black wolf jumps over the crowd at Marcas and chomps at his arm. At the last second, Marcas counters with a punch to the side of its head. It whimpers and falls limp to the ground.

Men and wolves keep coming at us in a never-ending tidal wave of attacks. One by one, my friends, my valiant protectors, are ripped away from my side. With all my might, I try to stay close, but the swirling commotion of the battle draws us further apart. Panic lodges in my throat as I frantically try to drudge my way back to them.

Wolves around me howl, snarl, and bite their enemy's legs with their piercing fangs, then drag them down to the ground while other pack members pounce.

The familiarity of the battle takes me back to that day in the forest when I thought a wolf would be the end of me. Not just any wolf. Conall. Fear shifts inside me, but I press it back down and clutch the amulet in my hand. I am not weak! I can fight! I am part wolf!

Through a gap in the action, I see the hooded figure slipping through the havoc like an unseen shadow, lurking in and around the mass of bodies, heading straight for me.

I suddenly feel small and pathetically helpless—exposed like a rodent trapped in the sights of a soaring eagle above.

Hurried movement to my right rattles me out of my trance. Swiveling at the precise moment, I cause Tavis to stumble forward rather than hook my arm like he intended. With my hands raised in front of me, I steady myself, poised and ready to defend.

He spits out a boisterous, jolly sort of mocking laugh as he rights himself. "You? Fight me? You think you're tough enough, huh? This could be fun." Excitement shifts in his narrow eyes as he clenches his jaw.

"Not as fun as you think," I mumble, scowling.

To the left and then right, we dance, moving in a circular motion. Lunges forward, trying to hit me, he misses. I counter with a punch to his side, also missing.

"Ooh, watch it! Don't let me get ya. Ah, I almost had you there. Huh, this is too easy!" He raises his eyebrows smugly, his lips puckered into a contemptuous smirk. And yet his efforts are halfhearted. A light punch. Then another. Again and again, he flails his fists in mockery of my skill. But while Tavis taunts me, I study his strategy, his combat maneuvers, and his flaws, just like Sam had taught me.

Tavis' biggest weakness is believing me to be a pathetically easy target. Big mistake. When he fakes his step again, instead of flinching like before, I grip his forearm and fling him over my shoulder with full strength, his body slamming hard on the ground. Victory—textbook annihilation! I grin, knowing Sam would be proud. Tate too.

While Tavis gasps for air, I chuckle. "I bet you didn't see that coming."

His eyes clamp shut as he rolls around, groaning and holding his ribs. I grin wider, knowing several must have cracked on impact.

As I look around to find my escape, my eyes lock on the cloaked stranger, now only a few feet away. Having used Tavis' weak attempt at capturing me as a diversion, they have advanced significantly, despite the crowded battlefield. They lift their arm and pull their hood back, finally revealing their identity. I gasp, seeing before me a slender-faced, beautiful woman with flawless ivory skin, high cheekbones, and dark red lips pressed in a thin line.

Conall's secret weapon is a woman?

A slight titter leaves me at the irony of it, but then recognition burns brightly within me. Her hair, those eyes—I've seen them before! The other woman—the one from my vision!

The amulet under my shirt sparks with heat against my skin, as though it too recognizes her.

As though we are the only two people around, she glides to me, her long ebony hair sashaying behind her as her brilliantly blue eyes seduce me into submission. As she stretches out her hand to seize me, Marcas tugs me away.

"Ve-Vevina?" he gasps, his eyes wide.

CHAPTER 6

Thicker Than Blood

Vevina flings her robe over her shoulder. When it floats to the ground, it exposes her slender, muscular body outfitted with tight dark-brown leather pants and a shirt with braided straps crisscrossing over the breastplate.

"Marcas," she replies flatly as though they are nothing more than acquaintances.

"How—" His eyes blink intensely. "You're . . . alive? We thought you were dead!"

A smirk crosses her lips. "Oh, I am very much alive."

For a moment, a flicker of joy shines brightly on Marcas' face before the dark shadow of understanding shifts his features flat. "You're with Conall."

Niall suddenly growls to my left, charging full speed at a brawny man. Getting punched in the process, Niall doubles over, coughing and wheezing. Then he gets up and lunges at the guy, taking him out at the knees. He crashes to the ground, where Niall pummels him with a barrage of punches. I almost feel sorry for the guy.

"I wouldn't expect you to understand, Marcas," Vevina continues, her tone smooth, like a scalpel slicing through flesh.

"H-how could you do that to me—to your family? All this time—with him. After what he's done to us!"

"What about what we've done? Father stealing his birthright! Turning our people against them. Denying his father the right to eternal rest with his own clan! If you want to blame someone, then blame Father!"

"How dare you defile his name? Daragh's the one who started this! Plotting to kill Father and take his place. And you stand there, justifying his actions!" Marcas says while pushing one of Conall's men away who tries to attack him. The man then drops toward Vevina.

"Did you ever stop to think maybe it's all a lie?" She hisses back, also shoving the man away with disgust. He stumbles and drops where he then stays.

85

"Back for more?" Sam hollers to the far right of me as he and Luc stand back-to-back, brawling with five men and several wolves. One of the wolves yelps and scurries back when Luc gives it a roundhouse kick to the torso.

Finn and Jamie are nowhere to be seen. Worry tugs at me.

"What does it matter anyway?" Vevina huffs with a snarl. "I've found where I belong and am better for it!"

"Conall!" Marcas growls.

"At least he knows what the rest of us want! Isn't stuck in the past, living the life our parents forced on us. You could see it, too, if you weren't blinded by a love for these—" She glares at me with repugnance. "—filthy humans!"

"You once believed as we do! How do you just walk away like that?"

A shadow of remorse flashes across her face, but then it vanishes. "It doesn't matter. Just accept it. Now, hand her over!"

"No!" Marcas blocks her with his arm.

"Don't make me kill you!"

"What's happened to you? The Vevina I knew wouldn't hurt anyone. Please, I beg you, Vevina, don't do this! It's not too late. Come back with us! We'll help you."

She throws her head back, her silky black hair flowing like water over her shoulder. "Who says I need help? Conall's good to me. Takes care of me." Her eyes narrow into slits of resentment. "More than you ever did!"

Marcas' shoulders slump. His beautiful green eyes look at her in pleading desperation. Then he looks at me. The agonizing torment I see makes my pulse quicken and my heart pound spastically. Would he give me up—forsake our love—for the chance to win back his sister from Conall's clutches?

In one effortless Herculean movement, Sam takes down two wolves synchronously with the swing of his arm, then whips around and joins Korin, in wolf form, rushing toward us—only to have their path blocked by several more of Conall's men.

Tate, combating near us, delivers a blow to a gigantic man the size of a small giant and sends him flying across the field, landing on top of a large rock. Wearing a triumphant smile, Tate then comes and stands near me.

Marcas breathes out hard as he stares at me with mournful, doleful eyes. They then shift into a stern look of disdain. He lifts his shoulders and turns. Glaring at Vevina, he says with absolution, "So be it."

Vevina lurches forward and grabs Marcas. He pushes me toward Tate as she spins Marcas around and tries to throw him into the trees. He reverse-steps her move, making her tumble to the ground. She gets up, panting from her efforts.

"You've been training," she says smugly, wiping her hair from her face. "Good thing, so have I."

She calmly maneuvers around Marcas.

"What's he promised you?" he asks as he turns with her every step.

"Freedom," she says without pause. "*Power!*" Her eyes widen, the words floating off her lips as though they hold their weight in gold.

"He can't give you that. You know how it works."

"Who says he can't?"

Marcas' face hardens. "He would have to—?"

"Exactly! You actually think he gives a damn about her?" She nudges her head toward me. "The crown's mine! My birthright. Not hers—not yours!"

She grabs Marcas' arm, but he pulls back. She sweeps her leg to trip him, but Marcas jumps out of the way like he saw it coming ages ago.

"Then it *was* you in Shae's vision!" he says, dodging another strike from her.

Vevina steadies herself and gradually turns to face us, grinning an evil snarl. "So, she already knows it belongs to me!"

The amulet ignites with nearly unbearable fiery heat, vibrating against my skin. It calls to me, declaring solidarity with only me in every wave of energy it pulsates through me. I am who it wants, not her.

Moving out from behind Tate, I take a step toward Vevina. "Your mother gave it to me—in my vision. Even when you tried to take it, she refused you."

"Lier!" she growls.

"See for yourself."

Vevina's fierce eyes narrow in on me as I take the amulet from under my shirt.

"If she wanted you to have it, then you would."

"Give it to me, now!"

"Vevina, stop this!" Marcas pleads. "The amulet chose Shae. You can't change fate."

"Like hell I can't!" Vevina charges me, but Marcas spins her around while Tate smoothly guides me out of the way. "She promised me! I am to rule!"

"Not how you think," Tate says, shoving a guy away, trying to get through to me. "You were promised to one of us. Our fathers agreed. Years ago—long before—"

"You lie!" Vevina screams, charging at him. He hits her arm away and pivots around, keeping me behind him the whole time.

"What reason would I have?"

"Uh, because you're pathetic!"

Conall, having battled his way back to us, shoves the last of his men out of his way and stands next to Vevina.

"My Lord!" She bows rigidly.

"I am not pleased, Vevina. You have failed me."

"But it's one against many. How can I—"

"Have I not trained you? Are you not capable of taking a life? Even that of your brother?"

She scowls and clenches her jaw. "Yes, my Lord. I can do this."

"But it seems you *cannot*," Conall says bluntly, emphasizing his last word with disgust. Then he shifts himself away from her. "I grow tired, Marcas. Let this be done."

Vevina lets out a monstrous scream as she shoves Conall to the side and sprints at me. Marcas punches her shoulder, making her whip around him. But it doesn't stop her from diving into the air toward me. Tate shoves me to the side and kicks Vevina in the stomach. She gasps for breath, landing on the ground with a heavy thud, then doesn't move.

Conall huffs and shakes his head.

Stirring sluggishly, Vevina rises to her feet. Tate grips her arms around her back. She tries to rip herself away, but when she can't, she spits at him.

"Nice behavior for a woman," he taunts. "Sort of glad you turned. I wouldn't want to come home to your hideous mug every night."

"Conall! Do something!' She screeches as she struggles.

He looks at her, his eyebrows in a deep vee. "No. No, I don't believe I will."

"Conall!" Vevina gasps, her eyes wide. "You and me, remember?"

His eyes turn cold and hollow. "Poor, naïve Vevina. You couldn't have possibly thought we'd end up together. Oh, but you did, didn't you? Sorry to disappoint, but it was never you, my dear. Always been Shae—what's best for the future of my kingdom, you know."

Tears stream down Vevina's face as she glares hard at him.

He raises his eyebrows and shrugs, then looks at Marcas. "Shae—now!"

Marcas steps in front of me as the battle rages around us. It is as though we exist on a different plane than the rest.

"I won't ask again. Give Shae to *me*!"

"Never!"

The hairs on the backs of my arms tingle as electricity builds, charging the air around us.

Conall's feet shift on the grass. His eyes, locked on Marcas, narrow in on him as the corners of his lips curl slightly.

Korin and Sam, having dealt with their attackers, come over. Now human, Korin gently takes my arm to move me away from Marcas. I resist at first, not wanting to leave his side, but the loathsome look in Conall's eyes stirs panic in me that I can't ignore.

Conall dives forward, transforming into the enormous wolf from my nightmares. Marcas swiftly leaps at him, morphing in mid-air and slamming into him with a booming thud. Violently gnashing their teeth, they crash to the ground. Marcas bites Conall's shoulder hard and shakes ferociously, making Conall yelp and thrash about.

Managing to get loose, Conall darts to the side, turns around, and then shakes himself off. Tufts of fur and dirt float away as he spreads his legs wide, his tail erect like a flag behind him. He lowers his head, exposing his gruesome grill, as though giving a taunting smile.

From deep within, Marcas lets out a billowing growl and bares his pointy teeth. His piercing, predatory eyes focus on Conall as if to convey that he will not back down.

Conall picks up his front paw and stomps it on the ground. Marcas retorts with a menacing, snarling snort, then the gnashing of teeth. Conall bounds forward, chomping at Marcas' feet. Marcas strikes back with a bite to Conall's ear. They both miss, then whip around, ready to go again.

With unrelenting force, Conall drives his attacks on Marcas, one after another. And with almost effortless movements, Marcas thwarts every maneuver like he'd been expecting it.

As I watch, fear courses through me like an adrenaline junky falling to their death. I cannot stop this madness, even if I try. I feel helpless—afraid Marcas could get hurt. Or worse.

Marcas wrestles Conall to the ground, pinning him on his side, only to have him reach around and nip at Marcas' hind leg, forcing him to jump back. Rising swiftly, Conall pounces on Marcas, knocking him backward and slamming him fiercely to the ground. Conall then pins Marcas down with his heavy front paws on his chest.

Panic jumps into my throat as I grip Korin's arm.

"Move, Marcas! Faster!" Sam hollers, cupping his hand around his mouth.

Snapping his head around, Marcas chomps his strong jaw at Conall's feet and legs. Catching one in his mouth, Marcas clenches down, making Conall wail out in pain as he plunges to the ground.

Sam cheers excitedly.

Yet again, Conall manages to wiggle himself out and scrambles to his feet, then comes at Marcas who zigzags just as Conall tries to jump on him.

Stifling a scream, I hold my breath. Will Marcas prevail? Or will this battle be the end of happiness as I know it?

Marcas and Conall collide again. Up on their hind legs, they vigorously clack their teeth and kick and scratch at one another, trying to bring each other down. Marcas thrashes Conall's head to the side with a swing of his paw, then digs his teeth into his neck before wrangling him ferociously to the ground. Conall lets out a long howl, then whimpers as his body slumps.

Breathing heavily, Marcas pauses, Conall's neck clenched in his jaw. Then he listlessly opens his mouth and drops Conall, who lands on the ground in a heap. Blotches of crimson blood are visible on his neck.

There is no movement from Conall. Not even the shallow rise and fall of his chest with a single breath.

Though men and wolves still battle all around us, it is as though all sound has refused to pierce the scene.

Is Conall really dead; gone for good, to never torment us again? My heart leaps into my throat as I breathe frantically. A sinking feeling shifts my joy to fear. What does this mean for Marcas? Is it murder or self-defense? Do their laws justify defending one's kingdom? Or could he be imprisoned for such a defeat?

Marcas lets out a yelpish growl and a snort as he walks to Conall and sniffs, then nudges the lifeless body with his muzzle. His ears perk up, then flop.

Raising his head, Marcas trills a long, drawn-out howl into the sky. The haunting undertones portray a song of loss rather than victory.

To take a life, no matter how wretched the person may be, must leave one forever haunted by it.

The war around us ceases.

With his head and ears low, Marcas turns and dallies toward us, sadness running deep in his soulful eyes.

"Look out!" Korin roars. But it is too late. Having leaped into the air, Conall lands on Marcas' back, biting down hard on his shoulder with his razor-sharp teeth. Marcas lets out a piercing howl as Conall thrashes him back and forth, then down to the ground. Grass and dirt fly into the air, creating a dust cloud that momentarily hides them from view.

"No!" I scream so fiercely that my throat burns. Korin holds me back, but panic and fear already pin me where I stand.

Bright, scarlet blood smears through Marcas' fur as Conall rips and tears at his flesh. The more Marcas kicks and struggles to escape, the more the blood spreads.

"Sam, you mustn't interfere!" Korin warns, grabbing his arm. "He must do this on his own. It's the only way."

Sam swears under his breath and screams out his anger as he turns and punches one of Conall's men standing behind us.

Marcas makes one last pull to break loose before falling limp. Conall growls and gives a vigorous shake before releasing his grip. Then he prances around Marcas' motionless body as though doing a victory lap.

"Please, Marcas, please!" I cry under my breath as tears stream down my cheeks. "Don't leave me . . . I can't live without you!" Marcas' words, confessed to me that night outside Duke's, ring true to me now more than ever as I feel the crippling possibility of losing him forever. My heart tightens in my chest, taking my breath away. "Marcas, please get up." I sob.

A light whimper leaves Marcas as he moves, but he collapses back down when Conall snaps his teeth at him as he passes.

"Try again, Marcas," I whisper. "Get up. Please! You can do this!" With everything I have in me, I send courage and strength to him through our connection. If he feels even the slightest bit of it, he will know we are in this together. He can do this; I know he can.

Lethargically, Marcas lifts his head and searches for me through the crowd. When our eyes meet, hope sputters to life inside me. I breathe deep and magnify strength and love to him across the distance between us. "I'm with you, Marcas. Always and forever," I whisper. His ears perk up, making my heart patter in reply. "Yes, Marcas! Get up. Fight! Take him down!"

Shifting his legs underneath his body, Marcas tries to get up again. This time when Conall gnashes his teeth at him, Marcas does not relent, rising to a stand. Firmly on all fours, he steadies himself and blocks Conall's path.

Conall lowers his head and growls, exposing his blood-stained teeth as a reminder of what he's capable of.

As Marcas stomps a step forward he lets out a monstrous bark, seeming to rise from within him with the intensity of a thousand kings. The powerful sound ricochets through the clearing, silencing everything.

Chills run down my arms. "Now, that's an alpha." I grin through my tears at Korin, who is also smiling.

Baring his pointy teeth, Marcas snarls aggressively at Conall, forcing him to shrink back. But then he counters with a frenzied chomping clack of his teeth at Marcas' face. In retaliation, Marcas bites at Conall's ear, ripping it with his teeth, making him howl in pain to which Conall tries to sink his teeth into Marcas' backside. With a swift whip of his tail, Marcas whirls around and chomps down on the back of Conall's neck. Conall yelps sharply as he's forced to the ground and pinned flat on his side with Marcas' heavy paw.

Conall lets out a pleading whimper.

All are focused on them now. Even the birds have ceased their song in awe of Marcas' dominance over Conall.

Marcas reluctantly releases Conall's neck and straightens up tall, his paws still holding Conall down. But Conall does not get up. Instead, he squeaks out another blubber of whimpering whines while benevolently patting his front paw against Marcas' leg as though indulging in a playful game. But it's not Conall's submissiveness that exposes his defeat. Instead, it is his vile, cunning, and nefarious behavior—which everyone has seen—that reveals him to be the pathetically despicable coward that he is.

Marcas has won—courageously and with honor. And everyone watching knows it. Who will follow Conall now?

To prove dominance, Marcas reveals his teeth to Conall once more before releasing his weight and stepping back. Conall stays still, then slowly rolls onto his stomach. While his tail wags swiftly back and forth across the ground behind him, he keeps his head low, his nose almost touching the ground. Yet he does not look at Marcas standing over him. Then he scrambles to his feet. Marcas tries to nip at him, but he scurries off, his tail tucked between his legs.

Some of Conall's followers join him, while others disperse in different directions. Men from our side run after them while others cheer so thunderously that my ears ache.

Finn and Jamie are at the center of the field, yelling and cheering, hands fisted, arms in the air. Niall and Luc are hooting and hollering alongside them.

The nightmare is over.

Though relief rushes on me like a heavy cloud has been lifted, I feel trepidation creep in as I watch Conall run away. Defeated but not incapacitated, he will be out there to exact revenge on us whenever he feels like it.

"I knew he could do it," Korin says.

"Never doubted it," I reply as I look at Marcas, smiling.

With his back to me, Marcas simultaneously turns and transforms back into a human. With his weary-filled eyes, he looks at me and smiles, then staggers and collapses to the ground.

CHAPTER 7

Not Out Of The Woods Yet

My heart thuds wildly as I sprint to Marcas'
motionless body. Tears stream down my face as I skid
to a stop and drop to the ground next to him. Blood
saturates over half his dirty shirt on his right side. My
hand shakes as I carefully roll him over onto his back.
"Mar-Marcas!"

His eyes are closed, but he's still breathing.

Korin, Sam, Niall, and Luc come rushing in,
followed by Tate, still restraining Vevina. Finn and
Jamie run up two seconds later, along with a crowd of
men I don't know, nor, at this point, do I care.

Korin kneels beside me. "May I?" He motions to Marcas.

"Please! I—"

Korin begins to examine Marcas' extremities and his head. Then he rips off Marcas' shirt. Mangled bloody flesh is visible on his shoulder, the blood too thick and matted to see just how bad the injuries are.

Choking back a sob, I grip Marcas' hand and bring it to my chest. He lets out a soft groan. "Marcas!" I breathe. "I'm here!"

He moans again, trying to move.

"Stay still, friend. I've got you." Korin holds Marcas still with his hand on his torso. Then he turns to Sam. "We need a car. Now!" His harsh tone sends chills through me.

"On it. Hang in there, Marcas!" Sam says, then leers at Vevina when he speeds by, grabbing Finn. They run west at a dead sprint.

Other than the visible worry in his eyes, Sam seemed okay—only a gash with crusted blood over his right eyebrow, which will probably leave a wicked scar he'll happily brag about later.

"Call Kathryn," Korin says, looking at Niall. "Have her meet us at—" He turns to me.

"Yes, my house!" I say, in a rush, my words nasally.

Niall takes out his phone and makes the call.

I don't ask who Kathryn is, because if she can help Marcas and get to us fast, I don't care.

Marcas lets out a gritted gasp as he tries to move again. "How . . . bad is it?"

"You just stay still. We'll get you out of here soon," Korin says, then stares at me, his brow furrowed. Fear runs thick in his eyes.

Fresh, hot tears bubble in my eyes, momentarily blurring everything. I blink them away and sniff as I wipe them with the sleeve of my jacket.

Korin looks around. "We need a cloth or . . . something to stop the—"

"Here," I say, taking off my jacket and giving it to him. He presses it hard against Marcas' shoulder, making him wail in agony.

"I know, man, I'm sorry. Hang in there."

"Please, Marcas, stay with me!" Gut-wrenching fear grips me to the point where I can scarcely breathe. You cannot take him from me now that the nightmare is finally over. Please!

Moving to sit up, Marcas cringes and gasps.

"Marcas, no, stay still!" I cry.

"Easy," Korin warns as we shift Marcas to a seated position, resting against a boulder.

For the first time since Marcas collapsed, he sees me. His tired, green eyes blink while he struggles to smile through the pain.

Sniffing, I take a heavy breath and attempt a smile, but the more I try not to think of how bad

Marcas' injuries are, the more the tears force their way out.

Afraid of hurting him, I hesitate before gently caressing his cheek and wiping a smear of dirt away with my thumb. "You'll be all right, Marcas," I whisper. He just has to be. A tear trickles down my cheek to my chin, but I don't bother to wipe it away. Another one will be along shortly.

Marcas lazily closes his eyes, as if my touch brings him comfort. When he opens them again, he smiles wearily. "Are you . . . *hurt*?"

"I'm fine. Don't worry about me. Just don't . . . move anything."

"You . . . know me. I can't . . . help—" Inhaling sharply, Marcas curls over, his face turning pale.

Please, Sam, hurry!

"Lay back down, Marcas. Please!" I say, struggling to hold back sobs. I know he must feel the horrid feeling of doom I unwillingly send his way, but I can't stop the dark thoughts from entering my mind.

"Niall." Marcas pants.

"I'm here!" Niall says, his voice hiding a slight quiver in its baritone sound. "We're all good. Marcas, please."

Niall's shirt is torn, his clothes dirty, and his elbows skinned, but nothing appears serious, and I am extremely thankful for that.

While I adjust Marcas into a better position, a stout man with a weathered face, piercing black eyes, and muscular tribal tattooed arms walks up, stopping at Marcas' feet.

"Father!" Korin scrambles to his feet, but the man shushes him back down with his hand, then turns to Marcas.

"My Lord—Marcas," The man's voice is deep and scratchy. He bows reverently, his fisted hand covering his heart.

Marcas sluggishly peers up at him. "Thank . . . you . . . for coming."

"By my honor, I have done you wrong, my boy, and doubted the seriousness of the situation. Please forgive this misguided old man."

Marcas smirks a little. "You showed . . . up." Then he winces and grabs his shoulder but gets Korin's hand instead.

"We will fight this, Marcas, you and I. Stop this from happening to anyone else."

Breathing erratically now, Marcas can only nod slightly.

"Thank you," I say in his stead as I stand and extend my hand to the man, "for sending these men."

"Shae, I presume!" The man clasps his warm, firm hands around mine. "Delighted, my dear. I am Tynan."

"Korin and Tate's father, I know. Marcas told me about you." Nerves threaten to do me in, but I force them back with a gulp and a gentle smile. "If it wasn't for Korin and especially Tate, I don't know what would have happened," I say, glancing at Tate.

Tate grins at me sheepishly, to which Vevina rolls her eyes and squirms in his grasp.

"My Tate?" Tynan asks in astonishment. He looks at Korin, who smiles and nods, then at Tate with a smile of pride, bright and strong, on his face.

Tate stands a little taller and nods dutifully to his father.

"My boys," Tynan says happily as he glances around for one other. A shadow drifts over his face. When he faces me again, a hint of sorrow shimmers in his eyes. He squeezes my hand and peers deep into my eyes. The urge to look away is strong, but I resist. "I will do right by you and Marcas. My word, I will. Anything you need, just ask."

"Thank you."

"Now, to business." He releases my hands and walks to Tate. "What to do with you?" He snaps.

Bewildered, Tate opens his mouth to protest but stops short when his father turns to Vevina.

Tynan makes a triple-ticking sound with his mouth. "Disappointing, to say the least, young lady. Your father will be rolling in his grave at what you've become!"

"Whatever, old man. You think you've won?" She snorts a laugh. "Conall will claim what he deserves. He'll never give up!"

"Oh, for crap's sake, give it a rest, would ya?" Niall huffs. "Ooh, blobbity-blah-blah, Conall's so awesome! Sheesh—know when to quit a lost cause. He ain't comin' back for ya, sis. Ditched you like stale bread!"

Vevina kicks at Niall, but Tate pulls her back. She jerks her body to get free, but when he tightens his grip, she thrashers her shoulder at him.

A wave of muffled laughter carries through the crowd of men around us.

I would give anything to believe our situation is laughable, but I know better than to underestimate such a man. Conall is still out there. Still a psycho with a grudge. Whether it's to rescue Vevina or not, he could come back at any time and do the unthinkable to get what he wants. I am sure of that, now more than ever.

"What should we do with her?" Tate asks, struggling to wrangle her like a feisty, unruly dog at the end of a leash. He yanks her arms down. She growls in his face, then huffs and glares loathingly away.

"Feed her to the wolves." Niall grunts. "Serves her right."

Several soldiers, hauling small groups of what's left of Conall's men, put their fists to their chests in reverence toward Marcas as they pass. Too weak to return the gesture, Marcas raises a finger, his eyes barely open enough to see.

"Marcas should decide," Korin says, adjusting the pressure on Marcas' shoulder, which makes him scream out. "Sorry, man—but not in this condition."

"I—"

"No, Marcas. Not now. Not like this."

"It would be an honor to take over her watch," Tynan says. "To give you time to recover first."

Marcas weakly licks his lips, then scarcely says a breathy, "Yes," his breathing having become alarmingly shallow. It takes more effort than he has to give.

With the quick jerk of his head, Tynan directs two of his men to take Vevina from Tate. They drag her away without saying a word.

Kneeling beside Marcas, I put my hand on his leg. "Marcas, how're you doing?"

"Ti . . . I'm . . . tired."

"I know, but try and stay with me, okay?" Looking at Korin, I ask in a harsh whisper, "Where is Sam?"

In the distance, a high-pitched double beep of a car horn sounds.

Korin and a handful of Tynan's men lift Marcas' limp body into their arms and haul him from the field toward the sound of the honks.

Jamie grabs my arm, and we follow, with Niall, Tate, and Luc behind us.

CHAPTER 8

Falling To Pieces

Kathryn, the nurse the boys apparently have on speed dial, and now I guess me, too, lifts Marcas' wrist and puts two fingers against it, then checks her watch.

After a minute, she nods and says, "Good," before laying his arm next to his blanket-wrapped body.

On the chair in the corner, Tax lies in wait. Every so often, he lifts his head and lets out a whistling whimper. Then he puts his head back down, his eyes always watching Marcas.

Marcas' breaths are steady, almost appearing tranquille-esque, though I know a storm of torturous pain rages inside him.

"Will he be all right?" I ask.

"It'll take time. He's heavily sedated right now, so he can rest. I'll come back tomorrow to check on him."

"You're the nurse that helped me before, aren't you?"

Giving a smile, she then begins to gather her medical instruments.

Most likely Marcas' age, she's tall and thin with blonde hair and bright brown eyes.

"How do you know them?" I ask. The idea of another one of Marcas' past relations wandering around, pining for him, makes my stomach turn.

"We go *way* back."

How far back? Years? Decades?

"Oh, crazy, you're here too. Di-did you know they'd be coming here then?"

She looks at me with a hint of amusement, as if she is enjoying the awkwardness she's putting me through.

After zipping up her doctor's bag, she stops and looks at Marcas. The sigh she gives sounds more like that of a worried mother than the longing of an ex-lover.

"He's my cousin. Reckless and headstrong. But family nonetheless."

Cousin! Relief washes over me. "Oh! So, you're one of them. I guess I should have known. You didn't ask too many questions about his injuries. You live here, then?"

"For the moment. I go where I'm needed, and right now, that's here. He's lucky I didn't head north like I'd planned to."

"Thank you for helping him. And me when you did." I smile warmly at her.

"I'm glad to see you've recovered," she says, grinning, but then she frowns and looks at me more knowingly, sadness in her eyes. "Marcas' wounds are serious, Shae. Deeper than most of our kind can handle. If I hadn't gotten to him when I did, he might not have—" She stops, then firms up. "Don't let him out of this bed! I mean it. He'll try to, well before he should, but he needs rest—no matter how restless he gets. You tell him I said that!"

"I will," I say with conviction, though her declaration makes my stomach sink.

Before following her out of the room, I grab the bowl of pink-tinted water and the blood-stained towel on the nightstand.

She closes the door behind me and walks through the kitchen to the front door. She waves at me, then leaves.

A rumbling sort of huff-snort comes from the mound of blankets on the long couch, then the rustling and shifting of sheets on the queen air mattress in the center of the room. And then nothing but unmoving mounds of blankets, pillows, and heavy-breathing people sprawled out everywhere as if they lacked the energy to prepare a proper bed before falling into an exhaustion-induced slumber.

I wish I could do the same, but with Marcas' injuries so life-threatening, sleep is the furthest from my mind.

After pouring the contents of the bowl into the kitchen sink and tossing the towel in a bucket by the garbage can, I head back into my room. The door lets out a soft squeak as I close it with a click. Then, I walk to the chair at the side of the bed and sit down.

Marcas' shoulder is bandaged up, sticking halfway out from under the covers. There is no visible blood now, though, but I can't get the image of his lifeless, bloody body when they brought him in.

Shaking the horrible image from my mind, I focus on Marcas' breathing—in and out, steady and quiet.

I recall the last time I watched him sleep peacefully in this room. However, the circumstances were reversed, with me being the injured one. How spiteful I had been, seeing him in his serene state while my world felt like it was swallowing me whole.

But not now. Watching him, I am thankful to see him so calm and still. I would rather him stay this way and wake when he's healed than see him in such agony. Especially since I'm to blame. If I hadn't gone into the forest that day and made Conall hunt me down and take me from Marcas, none of this would ever have happened. Marcas would be whole, healthy, and in my arms at this very moment.

An overpowering blubber spills from my lips. I try to stifle it with my arm, but it doesn't stop the overwhelming wave of grief and regret that comes. Tears stream down my face, but I hardly care. The emotions, once held back by the need to make sure Marcas was safe, come crumbling down like a mudslide on a rainy day.

Marcas almost died! I bawl even harder, the reality of it ripping at my heart like nothing I've ever felt before. To lose Marcas would be as if I'd died myself. Never have I ever known such fear.

But he's here. Still breathing. Still mine. I must cling to that truth if nothing else.

As I blow my nose, I continue to cry, heaving sobs and snorts, not caring if anyone hears me. Who would fault me even if they did?

Tax gets off the chair and comes to me, putting his chin on my leg. "I'm okay, Tax." I sniff. In reply, he nuzzles his nose on my hand until I scratch his ears. "Everything will be fine."

Feeling the weight of the day pushing down on me and exhaustion from crying till there were no tears left to fall, I let Tax go back to the chair in the corner while I rest my head back on mine. With my arms folded over me, I shut my eyes.

Though my body is still, my mind and insides spin, lulling me into a whirling yet oddly satisfying, lethargic meditative state.

*   *   *

I wake with a start, regretting it the second I jerk my head, my neck stiff and stuck at an awkward angle against my shoulder. I hadn't moved for who knows how long. Massaging the tightness out, I gingerly bring my head to the center. All at once, the events leading up til now bombard my mind. In a panic, I seize Marcas' hand. Relief engulfs me. I feel warmth. He's still breathing. Still alive.

"I love you," I mutter aloud as I send my feelings through our connection. If anything, Marcas can at least feel it and know I am with him.

I feel a gentle, almost imperceptible squeeze of my hand in his. My heart patters. Tears of joy ripple in my eyes. "Marcas!"

Marcas groans quietly as he shifts in the bed, his eyes lazily rolling open. He blinks twice, then locks eyes with me. The corners of his lips turn up. "Mo Chroi!" He breathes.

Kissing his hand, I then touch it to my cheek and nod. "Yes, Marcas, I'm here! No, stop. Don't move!" I say, forcing him back down, but he sits up anyway, cringing when his shoulder touches the headboard.

114

His breathing is quick and aggressive. Though he tries to hide it with a smile, I know he's in significant pain.

"Please, Marcas, lay down."

"I wanted to get a . . . look at you."

I smile through my tears. "I'm not hurt. See, no scratches." I move from side to side, showing I'm not lying.

Seeing him this way breaks my heart. I want to take the pain away, but I can't. Regret forces more tears to flow from me.

"Shh, no crying," he says, reaching over to wipe them from my cheek, but he cries out when his shoulder moves.

"Marcas!"

"I-I'm fine."

Starting as a speck on his bandage, ruby-red blood spreads outward, saturating his shoulder in seconds.

"Sam!" I yell, my heart in my throat.

The door bursts open. Sam, followed by Finn and Niall, rush in. Korin stays at the door's edge.

"Help him!" I say, letting go of Marcas' hand to make way for Sam.

"Hey there, dude. You're not supposed to be moving. Doctor's orders," Sam says, looking from Marcas to the blood-soaked bandages. Then he looks at me. The trepidation I see in his eyes sends a chill through me. Focusing back on Marcas, Sam forces a smile. "Why don't you lay back down, Marcas? Get some rest."

Marcas pants to catch his breath. "Y-you all right?"

Korin moves quickly to Sam's side. "Of course. We all are."

"Just-just stop! Lye back down, Marcas, please!" The subtle panic in Sam's voice makes my heart lurch.

"Should I get Kathryn?" I ask.

Sam gives a rigid nod.

My hands shake as I take out my phone and text, *'Please, come quick. It's bad.'*

Two seconds later, a ping, *'Coming,'* comes in reply.

Gripping the phone in my hands, I hold my breath, wondering how long it will take her.

Marcas lets out an agonizing scream so loud that it shakes me to my core.

I rush to him, but Sam blocks me with his arm. The others race in to restrain Marcas, who's thrashing around violently.

Tax jumps off the chair, barking and howling loudly over and over.

"Jamie!' Finn yells. She comes running in as if waiting for his call. "Take Shae. Now!"

She grabs my arm and pulls me toward the door.

"And someone shut that dog up!" Sam yells.

"No! Marcas!" I shout and cry profusely. But Jamie does not let up, making me and Tax leave the room. "Marcas!" I yell as the door slams shut.

"Shae, there's nothing you can do! Let them take care of him."

"Get off me!" I growl, shoving her hands away from me as I glare at her. Then I break down, blubbering more.

"Shh, it's all right, Shae. Everything will be all right."

Falling to my knees in the middle of the kitchen, I wail into my hands with such exertion that my head throbs. Mascara-lined tears soak my cheeks, but I don't care about anything but Marcas. I am lost without him.

"No, no, please. . . not Marcas," I mumble into Jamie's shoulder as she pulls me close. Her body shakes as she cries with me. No longer barking, Tax snuggles up at my feet.

The front door bursts open, and Kathryn rushes to the bedroom, not bothering to say a word when she passes. The door bangs closed again as if sending a message of my future straight to my heart—forever shut out of a life with Marcas.

Every painstaking minute feels like an eternity. Hearing Marcas' piercing screams torments me unbearably—cries for help I'm incapable of answering.

"What are they doing to him?" I cry, heaving in a breath. "Please, Marcas, please be okay." With my knees tucked to my chest and my arms wrapped tightly around them, I rock back and forth. In a trance, I watch the door, waiting, begging for it to open again; to have Marcas walk out and be all right.

Jamie strokes my hair softly, her other hand resting gently on mine.

The horrific screams abruptly stop, filling the house with an eerie silence. Chills scatter across my body as an uneasy feeling shifts in my gut.

Once again, the door opens.

Pale-faced, with blood on their hands and clothes, Finn, Sam, Niall, and Korin exit the room. Sadness glistens in their tear-filled eyes.

"*No!*" I wail at the top of my lungs as all feeling leaves my body. "No-n-no!"

Rushing to me, Sam drops to the floor and tries to wrap his arms around me, but I shove him away. "I did this to him. He-h-he's dead because of me!"

CHAPTER 9

How To Move On

"Shae!" Sam grabs my shoulders and shakes me, forcing me to look at him. "He's all right, Shae! He'll be all right!"

"Wh-What?" Tears run down my cheeks. "Marcas—"

"There was a tooth embedded in his shoulder. Caused an infection, but we got it." Sam's weary, tearful face brightens with a smile.

Hope flutters in my heart. I grab Sam and hug him, squeezing so tightly that he laughs and winces at the same time.

"I wanna see him!" I say as I let go of him and get up.

"I'm not sure that's a good idea. There's blood and—"

"Sam, I don't care. Please! I have to know he's alive."

He looks at Kathryn, who's leaning on the back of a kitchen chair.

She shrugs. "If you're gonna do it, do it now. You only have a couple of minutes before the meds kick in."

I rush to the door but then stop. I know what I said before, but dread of what awaits me on the other side suddenly keeps me from turning the knob. I look back at Sam. He smiles warmly at me, his eyebrows raising as he nudges his head for me to go. Swallowing hard, I turn back to the door, open it, step through to the other side, and close it behind me.

The small lamp on the nightstand illuminates Marcas' pale, tired face with an orangish hue.

"Come . . . here," he says breathlessly, reaching out his hand to me. Substantial blotches and smears of blood are all over him, the sheets, and the blankets covering him. It reminds me of a crime scene photo from a murder documentary. I try not to focus on it as I move closer to him and sit on the edge of the bed.

"I'm so sorry, Marcas!" My eyes well up with tears. The grief I've been suppressing for having almost lost him spills freely from me.

Marcas grabs my hand. A slight smile crosses his lips. "Mo Chroi. . ."

"No." Shaking my head, I gasp for labored breath. "It's all my fault." I sniff. "You almost died because of—"

"Conall, Shae. Not you. Never you."

"But I—"

"Don't you see? He failed. Not even death can . . . come between us," he says, then coughs.

I know Marcas is right. Even when death seemed inevitable, we still prevailed. But no matter the degree of separation you want to put on it, I still played a part.

"I thought I'd lost you!" I say with a stuttered breath.

He shakes his head slightly. "Never . . . my love." Then his eyes slowly close, his head sluggishly settling against the pillow.

Taking a deep breath, I exhale long and slow, flushing out the pent-up feelings of angst I've been clinging to. We are safe now. I feel it in my bones. Yet a sliver of fear still remains. Who will come to challenge us next?

As I watch the mesmerizing rhythmic rise and fall of Marcas' chest, my mind drifts to the past, and the strange turns my life has taken. I no longer feel like the victim of a broken heart. Trapped by a belief that love should be earned and not freely given. Marcas' love has changed me forever. It lifts me up and makes me want to be a better person. It is real love. Powerful. Pure. A love I can neither deny nor take for granted. I have finally found myself—found my purpose and where I belong. I have found my fate.

Leaving Marcas to rest, I return to the kitchen.

Kathryn is at the table, typing something into her phone. She puts it down and looks at me. "He asleep?"

I nod and pull a chair out, then sit down. "I'll wash him and change the sheets when he's more stable."

"Sorry about the mess. I can't—missing a tooth!" She blinks rapidly and wipes a tear from the corner of her eye. "Guh, seriously, I'm better than that."

"It's not your fault." I smile to reassure her, yet I know she will still beat herself up for it no matter what I say. Because that's what I'd do. "I'm just grateful you were here. I wouldn't've been able—"

She reaches over and grabs my hand on the tabletop. "You're capable of so much more than you realize, Shae. Marcas is lucky to have you. He needs someone strong by his side. I heard you held your own out there. Gave Tavis a run for his money." Giving my hand a gentle squeeze, she sighs, then lets go and sits back, chuckling. "I wish I'd seen his face. Did he cry? Please tell me he cried!"

Laughing, I sit back myself. "I wish. He definitely broke a few ribs, though."

"Are you talking about Tavis taking a ride over your shoulder?" Sam asks, moving across the kitchen from the living room. "Bam! Right on the ground." He laughs and opens the fridge. "Dude, where's the food?"

"Why don't you get off your butt and get some!" Jamie says, coming into the kitchen. "Sheesh. Not our job to feed you." She rolls her eyes, then winks at me as her lips curl into a playful grin. "You hungry, Shae? You haven't eaten. Hey Sam, do something useful, and take Finn and Niall to get me and Shae burgers."

"You read my mind!" Niall says, walking into the room, with Finn and Tate.

Tate gives me a hesitant smile. It dawns on me that I haven't seen him since we've been back. I wonder where he's been.

"Come on. Two burgers with extra crispy fries. Double the ranch," Jamie says, walking over to Finn.

He wraps his arms around her. "Oh really? Anything else?"

"Yeah, why don't you get yourself a little somethin-somethin while you're at it?" She clicks her cheek and winks playfully. "Kathy, you want anything?" she asks over her shoulder, then retracts and giggles when Finn teasingly nibbles at her neck.

Niall rolls his eyes.

"Not me. I've got things to do," Kathryn says, getting up. When she looks at me, her eyes weigh heavily with concern. "I'll come by about nine to change Marcas' IV and see how he's doing. Call me if you need anything."

Giving a smile, I nod, and she leaves.

"Anything else before I call it in?" Tate asks. When no one responds, he returns to the living room, where it's mostly quiet.

Grabbing a chair from the table, Sam moves to the center of the room and sits the wrong way on it. "You know, I've been thinkin'."

"Don't hurt yourself." Jamie grins, to which Sam snarls, his eyes narrowing slightly in annoyance.

"Seriously, though," he continues. "Funny thing about that battle? I saw a lot of familiar knuckles punchin' back at me." Sam grunts, casually looking at Finn. "Like Alex Gasnett. I thought he was back in Colorado. Nope!" Anger lingers in the last word.

Finn frowns. "Same with Roger McNab. And Mitch Westlin."

Sam scowls. "I'm getting damn sick of people we know switchin' sides."

The room grows silent, the unspoken names of Vevina and Ardan lingering in the air.

Sam suddenly pounds his fist on the top of the chair's back. "Really, Vevina? Couldn't find a better person to fake your death for? Makes me sick. At this rate, there'll be no one left to trust!"

Tate returns to the kitchen, and the room goes silent. "Food'll be ready at six."

"You guys go. Us girls will hang back." Jamie walks over to me and puts her hands on my shoulders, giving them a firm yet gentle squeeze. "Ooh and some onion rings!"

"Mmm, me too!" Niall says as he heads into the living room.

"Guys! You want 'em you order 'em 'cause I'm not calling again." Tate says walking to the front door. Jamie and I follow him.

"Finn will." Jamie winks, then kisses him before he goes out the door. She closes it behind him and walks to the long couch by the window and plops down on it.

As I sit next to her, I can hear the boys talking through the window as they get into the cars and drive away.

Through unfocused eyes, Jamie peers out the window, as if doing so will give her the answers to the troubling thoughts she seems to be keeping to herself.

I hoped Jamie had made it out of the whole hostage situation unscathed, but now I'm not so sure.

Grabbing the remote off the arm of the couch, I flick off the TV in the corner. "You wanna talk about it?" I whisper because anything louder would sound like yelling in a house as quiet as this one.

She turns and looks at me, her eyes shadowed with a look I can't quite read. "About what?"

"It might help, Jamie. It did for me when—"

"There's nothing to tell." She inhales deeply. When she exhales, she smiles wearily. "I mean, for captors, they weren't all that bad. It's just—" She looks out the window again. "How could Ardan do that? Think that I—"

"It makes me sick. Korin—he was wrecked."

Even after we've had time to piece together what's happened, the damage of betrayal and lies still shrouds our moving forward—for those who just met him and those who have known him for a lifetime. The ever-looming, unanswered question of why haunts us all.

Licking my lips, I shift my body slightly, debating whether or not to ask my next question. But I must know, "How, uh . . . how did they get you?"

Her eyes shift to her lap, where she picks at her cuticles. "They used the old *I'm having car trouble out back* trick, needing a jump. And, of course, I fell for it. I'm such an idiot!"

"You didn't know."

"I should have—if I'd just listened to you."

126

"Did they hurt you?"

She shakes her head. "Just minor scratches when they shoved me in the trunk." She looks down at a long, red mark on the back of her forearm.

"You must have been so scared!"

She chuckles lightly and smiles. "You know me. I can handle anything."

Her blasé attitude would be convincing, but her wistful eyes give her unease away.

Conall's deep, piercing, angry tone echoes in my mind. I don't care how brave you think you are; that man's wrath breaks through all.

Putting my hand on hers, I give a slight squeeze. "But if you couldn't, it'd be understandable."

She shrugs, dismissing the fear and frustration she doesn't want to face. I don't blame her, but she can't hide from it forever.

"I mean, you know, we can't always be badass all the time." I smile a teasing grin, yet I hope she gets my meaning.

This time, her eyes smile along with her lips. "Some of us can! Taking Tavis down! *Whaaat*?"

"Never knew what hit him." I smile wide. "Me? Some fragile, weak thing. Hah, sorry to disappoint. *Shablam*! I flipped him so hard on his back he had to have seen stars." I laugh.

"Seriously! A ba-bye, dude!" She laughs. "But how'd you do it? He's huge!"

"That's right, you don't know! The amulet transformed me."

"Wha-seriously? Like a full-on wolf?" Jamie's eyes glimmer with excitement.

"I wish! I only get strength. Well, I shouldn't say *only*. You should have seen me throw Tate across the yard." Laughing, I mimic the distance with my arms. "So far!"

"Man, I would have paid to see that!" We laugh, then slowly, our cheerfulness shifts to somberness when we remember the reason she'd missed it.

"What about Marcas letting you go? What's that about?"

"Are you kidding? He can't tell me what I can and can't do! Not save my best friend? Yeah right!"

"Dang! You said that?"

I nod, giving a proud grin.

"Wow! And he agreed?"

"Pshaw, no." I laugh. "He definitely said no. But then changed his mind when I transformed."

"I'm-I'm sorry I missed all that." Sadness lingers in her eyes, even though she grins slightly.

"I know. And if you do decide to talk, I'm here, okay? Always. Or I guess there's Finn."

She smiles warmly and pulls me into a tight hug. Then she sighs as she lets me go and shifts herself to face the room. "Oh, hey, thanks for Marge. Quick thinking about the flu."

"Yeah, it seemed a viable enough reason for your unexpected departure since you already called in sick before."

"So, what's the plan now?"

"Life as usual, I guess."

"Seriously?" She laughs sardonically. "There's no going back after all that."

A part of me feels the weight of her words like a foreshadow of my undetermined future. Marcas and I are together; in it forever. But that doesn't mean others won't try to destroy what we want for ourselves. Won't do what it takes to shift the fates and mess everything up again.

"Normal, what even is that?" I sigh.

"I hear Finn and the others are headed to Duke's tomorrow." Jamie's eyebrows pulsate up and down rapidly. "That's normal, right?"

"That it is." I smile wide, believing a little fun is probably what everyone needs right about now. "But I'm gonna stay. Marcas, he's not better."

Her face turns somber. "But he will be, Shae." Then the corners of her lips subtly rise to meet her cheeks. "Especially if you keep playing nursemaid like you do."

"Stop it. He's in no shape."

"You wanna bet?"

The front door swings open, thankfully ending the conversation before my face turns too red to hide.

Jamie jumps off the couch and intercepts Niall at the door. "Where's my fries? I need me some crispy goodness."

"Would you—get back, you animal! Sheesh. Ya can't wait till I'm through the door?" Niall grumbles, tugging the bags from Jamie's clutches.

"Geeze, hangry much?" She moves out of his way and grabs drinks from Finn's full arms when he walks through the door. They move to the kitchen. Sam follows behind them. Tate's the last one through the door, closing it behind him.

"Where's Korin?" I ask, getting off the couch.

"Meeting with my father. Luc's there too. Conall should've never underestimated the kid. He's spilling all his brother's secrets."

"Serves Conall right! So that's where you were earlier? With your dad?"

He nods contemplatively.

"How'd that go?"

"Actually, we had a decent conversation for once."

"Really!"

He shrugs. "I mean, we're not besties yet or anything, but it's a start."

I laugh. "Besties, hmm."

"You know what I mean. Anyway, I was trying to relate."

"To who? Jamie!"

We both laugh.

"Dude, where's my bacon burger?" Sam yells from the kitchen. "You better not have forgotten it."

"Come on, you need to eat." Tate tips his head toward Sam's whiny voice, the rustling of paper bags, crinkling of tissue paper, and the squeaking of straws being inserted into plastic lids.

CHAPTER 10

The Wait Is Worse Than The Bite

The back wheels of the shopping cart make a piercing, rhythmic squeak as I maneuver around the display at the end of the aisle.

"Hey, you think these are any good?" Jamie asks, holding up a package of veggie burgers.

"Who for? The boys won't eat that."

She huffs and says under her breath, "Well, maybe it's not for them."

"You'd eat it?"

"Hells no!" She snarls and tosses it back on the shelf. "They're just on sale. These guys are gonna eat us out of house and home, you know. And we can't keep getting takeout. I've gained like ten pounds in two days!"

Niall whips the top half of his body around the shelving unit at the end of one of the aisles labeled *Chips* and *Candy* and holds up a bag of fiery cheese clusters. "Hey, can I get these?"

"No!" Jamie and I say together. He pouts and disappears back around the corner.

"Why'd he even ask us? Don't they have their own money for crap like that?" Jamie asks, examining other frozen food items in the same bay as the veggie burgers.

"He's sixteen, Jamie; give him a break."

"Try *sixty*! And I ain't his mommy." She snorts, then cringes. "Sorry, that was harsh. We about done here?"

Looking down at our full cart, I mentally check off the meals we've planned for. "Just need milk and eggs."

We move toward that section of the store.

Finn is eyeing the cuts of meat in the glass case at the butcher block at the back of the store when we walk up. The short, thick fellow with glasses standing behind the counter wearing a white apron covered in dark maroon blots of dried blood hands him a package wrapped in white paper. "Thanks, man!"

"You ready?" Jamie asks, sliding her arm around Finn's when he puts the meat in the cart.

He nods. "Steaks for Marcas. I'm sure he'll be ready for solids when we get home."

"You're gonna cook that first, right?" Jamie looks at it with disgust.

"Nope, the rarer the better." Then Finn laughs when she makes a gagging sound.

"Does it usually take this long to heal?" I ask while turning the cart sharply, forcing Jamie and Finn toward the dairy case.

Finn's forehead creases slightly. "No, but he'll get there. I wouldn't be surprised if he's out of bed when we get home."

"He better not be!" I open the cooler door and grab the milk and eggs. "I told Sam not to let him."

Jamie and Finn laugh.

"Fat chance he listens," Jamie adds, taking the items from me and adding them to the cart.

Korin and Tate walk up, hands full of odds and ends to add to the lot. "This should do it," Korin says, smiling.

"Niall! Hut two. Let's go, man!" Finn hollers over the aisle.

Everyone but Korin and I go outside to wait. When we reach the register, I spot Maggie behind the counter and nearly swallow my tongue.

"Shae." She nods and gives me a quick smile. Then she shifts to Korin. "Paper or plastic?" she says breathlessly. Her widened eyes sparkle while a smoldering grin covers her face.

"Plastic is fine." He gives a quick, pleasant smile back.

She refuses to take her eyes off him as she blindly grabs for things on the belt. "Nice day, huh?"

Korin looks at me as if I'm supposed to answer, but it's him she is staring at.

"Oh, uh . . . yeah, I guess it is."

She grabs several bags of chips and scans them. "Having a party?"

Korin shifts nervously. "Not really, just hangin' out."

"Ooh fun!" She squints her eyes cheerfully.

This perky, twitterpated look on her leaves a sour taste in my mouth.

Korin reaches into his back pocket, pulls out his wallet, retrieves a credit card from inside, and hands it to me. "Meet you at the cars." Then he leaves.

"Have a great day!" Maggie quickly yells, but he's already out the door. "Interesting. Moved on already?" Maggie asks as she scans, then bags more of our stuff. "I mean, not that I'd blame you." She bites her lower lip and watches Korin converse with Finn and Jamie outside. "Who is he?"

Jamie, standing with her back to us, whips around, scowling.

Maggie snarls, then continues scanning.

"He's Marcas' friend, Korin, from out of town," I say, wondering if I should have given such information so freely. The look on Maggie's face screams *Yay, new play toy!*

"He's yummy."

Ignoring the comment, I grab a pack of gum and toss it on the belt as the store door opens behind me. A moment later, Jamie is by my side.

"Maggie, nice to see you've finally joined the lower-working class. Good for you! Depot work, I hear, is very satisfying." She gives a snarky smirk.

Maggie scowls. "Total's $176.82."

While I pay, Jamie takes the groceries outside.

"'Hey, uh, does Korin have a girlfriend?" Maggie's eyes shift from me to the store's front window, then back.

I shrug. "Never came up." But that's never seemed to stop you before. "You should go for it."

"You think?" she beams.

I shrug and tap Korin's card on the console in front of me. "To be honest, I have no clue what his type is." But her being human could be the deal-breaker he can't get past. That or her being Marcas' ex. "But you'll never know unless you ask, right?" I smile.

She returns the gesture and hands me my receipt. "Yeah, maybe I will."

Giving a wave, I turn and go out the door.

Jamie and Korin are the only ones waiting when I reach the cars. "Huh, where'd the others go now?"

"Candy store." Jamie and I say at the same time.

Giving an eye roll, I laugh. "Seriously. Bunch of kids."

Korin laughs.

As we load the back of my car, I hear my name being called repeatedly from a short distance away. Looking up, I see Judy, my mom's friend and the town's biggest gossip, trotting to us from across the street.

"Whoops, look out," Jamie says, skidding to a stop, then hurriedly rounds the other side of the car to remain within earshot but nowhere near close enough to get caught in Judy's gossip radar.

"Oh, goodness, I'm glad I caught you," Judy says, breathless. "I didn't think I'd make it." She laughs a little high-pitched sort of giggly chirp.

"Hi, Judy. How are you?"

"Good, good. I just want to see how you're doing. I haven't seen you and Marcas in eating fer a while. I hope everything's right between you two."

Tingles up my spine warn me of her intent. "Oh, uh . . . yeah, we're, uh, okay, I guess." Out of the corner of my eye, I notice Jamie keeping a close eye on us as she pretends to watch for someone.

"More than okay, I'd say," Niall mumbles, walking by, to which Jamie slaps his shoulder as he passes her.

He grumbles incoherently and takes the empty cart back inside the store.

Judy's eyes light up. "Oh really! Tha-that's good news indeed. Wonderful!" Her smile widens as if she can't wait to tell what she's just learned to anyone who'll listen. "Well, I'd best be off. See you soon!" She winks at me as she hurries away.

When Niall walks past me, I slap his arm. Wincing, he looks at me sharply. "Dude, what's you girls's problem?"

Scowling, I shake my head.

"Seriously?" Jamie rolls her eyes at him, then shoves him toward the back door of the car. "Get a clue."

He is still protesting his innocence when Finn and the others walk up to us, bags in hand.

"What'd he do now?" Finn snickers.

"Blabbed about Marcas and Shae to the one person not to. Now the whole town'll know."

Finn clicks his cheek. "Hate to break it to ya, cutie, but thems news is out!"

A rush of embarrassment zings up my arms. It was only a matter of time, but it still makes me ill to think people are talking about me behind my back.

"Nuh-uh!" Jamie scoffs.

Finn's eyes flick toward the grocery store, then back at her.

Jamie's eyes go ablaze. "I'm gonna kill her!"

"Jamie, leave her be. Besides, at this point, it could've been anyone." I say while loading the last of the groceries.

"Mind your damn business," Jamie mutters as she opens the passenger side of her car and gets in, then pulls the door shut with a loud bang.

Cringing, I shrug at Finn as we crisscross paths, then get into the cars and drive away.

Back at the cabin, Jamie and I let the others unload, then unpack the groceries in the kitchen. Of course, not without protest first.

"How's he doing?" I ask Sam, whose head is resting on his arms on the kitchen table.

He sits up, huffs, and rolls his eyes. "Go see for yourself. Blah-ba-blah, on and on about getting out of bed. I nearly strangled him."

As I laugh, he gets up and puts a hand on my shoulder. "A saint you are, Shae. Truly." Then he walks away, shaking his head while snickers come from the others coming and going from the room.

Grabbing an apple off the counter, I then head into the bedroom.

Marcas is sitting upright in bed, flipping through a celebrity gossip magazine Jamie left lying around.

"Did you read the one about Justin and his co-host getting caught in the closet on set? Quite the scandal."

Looking up at me, he smiles. "I must have missed that one." Then he shuffles the pages.

Unable to tell if he's kidding or actually looking for it, I take the magazine from him, replacing it with the apple and ask, "How're you feeling?"

"Hey, I was reading tha—"

My eyebrow peaks at him as I sit on the bed and put the magazine to the far side of the nightstand.

"Guh, I need out of this bed!" he says, flinging the sheets off him. "Please, let me be done!" When he takes an aggressive bite of the crispy apple, juices spray into the air.

Tax, asleep in his now-favorite spot on the chair in the corner, snorts and puffs air from his mouth.

Giving Marcas a little nudge to move over, I then lay down. His sandalwood scent drifts into my nose when he moves the sheets out of the way. Even my pillows smell like him.

Chomping away at the last few bits of apple, he then tosses the core into the metal wastebasket by the door. It makes a ringing bong sound when it hits the side as it goes in. Wrapping his arm around me, he hugs me to his warm muscular chest and caresses his cheek against my head. "This is nice." He breathes out.

A broad grin forms on my face. "I've missed it too."

"Not more than I."

The rise and fall of his smooth, soft, bare skin on my face brings contentment, like walking through the door after a prolonged stay away from home. Peaceful. Inviting. Familiar.

"Thank you," he says quietly, "for taking care of me."

"Of course," I say, sinking into his comfort. "What else would I do?"

Lifting his hand, he tips my chin to see my eyes. "I mean it."

My cheeks flush with warmth. "I liked doing it. It made me feel . . . good."

"Oh, really, you enjoy me being incapacitated and weak." He snickers.

I laugh. "No, just vulnerable and real. More human for once." My hand moves to his shoulder, trailing the now-scarred skin. Only light pinkish areas remain, as though months old. I do not mind them. Sometimes we face challenges that leave scars, some visible and some within, but they all serve as proof that there is more to us than the pain we endured to earn them.

"Only with you, Mo Chroi," he says with a staggered breath as if my touch tickles in an appealing sort of way. Taking my hand, he aligns our fingers, then smoothly glides them together before resting them on his chiseled stomach. As he exhales, his breath ruffles my hair against my cheek.

"What?" I ask, knowing such a weighted sigh carries mounds of deep, unsettling thoughts.

"Who says there's something?"

"You forget; I know you."

"I fail to give your intuitiveness more credit. I was just thinking about this." He tilts my hand, showing me the ring on my finger.

"Marcas, no, not now. You're still recovering. We don't need to—"

"Excuse me, Shae, yes, we do." When he smiles, his emerald eyes dance with excitement. "I meant what I said. Why wait if we know what we want?"

Gulping down what ails me, I sigh. "I just don't want you pushing yourself. You were really hurt, Marcas. Lucky even to be alive!"

"Believe me, I know that. But something tells me that's not why you hesitate. Do you not want this, Shae?" he asks, caressing my arm.

"Yes, you know I do." I say lifting myself up on my elbow. "You think I'd go through all that if I wasn't? It's just . . . how do I tell my parents what you are? What if they freak out and think we're crazy and delusional and won't let us get married? Or worse, they do believe us and report you! Then the government comes and takes you to some secret facility and does all these tests and experiments on you and-and—"

"Shhh, Shae. Take a breath." He pulls me back down and holds me, his closeness somewhat subduing my overwhelmed mind. "It'll be all right."

Sinking into his arms further, I try to reassure myself that he's right. But the trepidity I feel runs deep, having kept me up till all hours of the night for one too many in a row. At least caring for Marcas has given me a better reason for the sleeplessness.

He looks down at me. "Why didn't you say something sooner?"

The concern in his eyes makes my heart sink. "It wasn't the right time."

"That shouldn't matter. If you have questions, or concerns, then talk to me—ask me! I can't help you if I don't know."

"I know, but I—you were—" His resolute eyes stop me from trying another excuse, so I nod and snuggle against his warm body like a safety net I desperately crave.

"All right, so let's figure this out. You're concerned about how they'll take it. So, then . . . we don't tell them."

"I already thought of that. But what happens when they're ninety and notice I haven't aged a day?"

"Blame it on bad eyesight."

His charmingly gorgeous lips, in a smirkish grin, try to pull a smile out of me, but I reinforce my frown.

"Marcas, seriously, they need to know. I won't live a lie."

"And I would never suggest that you do. Maybe we don't tell them right away then. We've done fine so far. Then, when it feels right, we will. And I highly doubt the government will get involved." He smirks.

"Okay, fine, whatever. Maybe not." I roll my eyes. "But seriously, how am I supposed to navigate things until then? Living in two different worlds—how does that even work?"

"Same way we've been doing it. And we'll come visit anytime you want. It's not like we're leaving forever."

"But we *are* leaving."

His lips press together in a tight, semi-frown. "For a while, yes. I've been away too long as it is. Besides, couples do it all the time after they're married."

"Yeah, but where to? I don't even know where you come from!"

"The forest." He grins coyly. But seeing the worry in my eyes, he stops. "Look, we'll have a place where your parents can visit. To them, we're just two regular people living normal lives, doing what all couples do."

"Who also happen to be wolves and the whole ruling for a few hundred years thing."

"You thought we lived like wild animals, didn't you?" He winks with more of a genuine sweetness to it than a tease.

"No, of course not," I huff, suppressing a smile because I believe that's exactly how they live every chance they get. But who's to say I won't also want that when times call for it? "All right . . . then what if we get married in secret like we need to, and stay a little longer until we have a chance to tell my parents about you and get married with them there? It would be another month, tops. Then we'll leave. Would that work?"

Marcas puts one of his bent arms behind his head while caressing my shoulder with the cool, soft fingers of his other hand. My thoughts drift toward other, more inviting things. But I force myself to stay focused.

"The thing is," he says after a minute, "when I marry you, Shae, I want it to be for real. I don't want to pretend we're not, for whatever reason."

My heart sinks. Neither do I. "Guh, then what do we do?"

"We plan them at the same time."

"Uh, no, that would mean telling my parents, like, tomorrow."

"What's wrong with that?"

"Nothing . . . It's just a little intimidating . . . and scary to be doing it again after what happened to me before." With my head against his upper body, I can hear his heart beating rapidly, more than usual; for the intensity of the topic or concern for it, I am not quite sure. "But I know time is short. The full moon is less than a month away."

"Shae, the last thing I want to do is push you into this before you're ready, but the longer we wait, the more danger you're in. Conall's gone, but that doesn't mean others won't try. And I don't want to risk you getting hurt." He squeezes me a little more. "But I understand. And just so you know, regardless of the circumstances, I can't wait to marry you and spend the rest of my life with you. But I will, if that's what you need me to do."

With my heart fluttering like a sparrow, I stretch up and kiss his lips. Their gentle firmness sends a spark of titillating energy rushing through me. I want to marry him—with all my heart, I do—but why am I also afraid? Looking into his eyes, I ask, "Two weddings at once?"

"Yes." He grins, never blinking.

"Do we even have time?" I ask, sitting up, my legs bent behind me.

"We'll make it work. It might mean sacrificing our free time for a bit, though, but it'll be worth it."

"And the boys?"

"We'd be doing it anyway, with or without a second one to plan. They're in, trust me."

His confidence inspires me, yet wedding planning does not succeed on enthusiastic optimism alone. Suddenly, the daunting task ahead of us overwhelms me. "Can't we stay in this tranquil, quiet place for a little longer before the crazy begins?" I ask, lying across his chest as I look at him.

"It won't be that bad."

"Uh, have you met my mom? Oh, wait." I laugh. "I guess not. Believe me, she wants this for me—like nothing else! It would not surprise me if she hired one of those fly-by planes to write *'My baby's getting married!'* in puffs of smoke in the sky."

"Fantastic! We'll save on postage!"

We both laugh.

My phone, on the bed next to us, buzzes a familiar, now haunting tune of foreboding. "You've got to be kidding me! Does she have a sixth sense or something?"

"Here, let me take it for you," Marcas teases, trying to answer the phone. Of course, I have to tackle him to get it back.

"Hey, Mom," I say, holding the phone to my ear as I sit up and try to calm my breathing. "What's up?"

"Oh, you know, I was just calling to see how you were. We haven't seen you in a few days. Everything going okay?"

"Yeah, it's all—"

"Let me tell her," Marcas whispers.

"All-all good here," I add, shoving his hands away because he keeps trying to grab the phone.

"You got company? I hear talking in the background."

"Just Jamie."

"Oh, right, okay. Well, if you don't have plans, we'd love to have you for dinner tomorrow night. Barbeque chicken."

"Sounds great, Mom. Want me to bring anything?"

"No, no, it's taken care of. Does six work for you?"

"Yep, I'll be there."

"Okay, then. Oh, I almost forgot. Bring that nice young man you've been seeing. It will be great to finally meet him."

A rush of cold blankets me.

"Okay, got to go; see you tomorrow. Love you, bye!"

The phone goes dead. My hand falls to my lap as I look at Marcas. The upturned corners of his lips push his cheeks up, crowding his sparkling eyes.

"What are you grinning at? They know! Man, Judy works fast" I grumble.

Sitting upright, Marcas adjusts himself closer to me. "I like a good barbecue." He grins triumphantly. "You up for that, my lady?"

Instinctively, I wrap my arms around his neck while he moves his arm around my waist. Clearing my throat, I ask, "The question is, are you?"

He laughs, his bright eyes dancing with eagerness. "Most definitely!" Then he kisses me, sending a shot of adrenaline through me.

Blushing so much that I can feel my skin heat up, I pull away and eye him, grinning. "Oh, we'll see about that."

CHAPTER 11

Into The Lion's Den

Pacing back and forth in front of the mirror in my bedroom, I then stop and stare into it one more time. The inkling to second-guess my outfit for the third time tugs at me.

Half expecting Niall to appear in the doorway to tease me about it, I look through the reflection for him, but he's not there. No one is. The house is empty. Having it be for the first time in days, I thought I would feel relief—peace. However, it feels empty in an unexpectedly lonely sort of way. Though they only left this morning, I miss them already.

At least they were nice enough to clean up before they went. I wouldn't have cared if they hadn't. Then, at least, there would be proof they'd been here in the first place. Now, it seems as if the last few days had been a distant dream or imagined scenario in my head.

Nonetheless, I am thankful for the time we were able to spend here together. Our bond has grown because of it. And Marcas and I have managed to leap over yet another obstacle in our way and come out better for it. At least that's what I tell myself, now feeling more alone than I have in months.

Coming from the other room, I hear a fast double knock at the front door before it opens. My heart quickens.

"Shae?"

"Back here!" I sigh. Why am I disappointed? I knew Jamie was coming.

She enters the room and stops. "Wow! You look great! Are you excited?"

"I'm not sure I'd say that."

"Ah, come on. Get it over with, and then let the wedding fun begin!"

"Uh, no, we agreed to tell them soon, but not today. No way."

"But I thought Marcas wanted—"

"Nope," I say, giving myself one last look in the mirror before turning and walking to the bedroom door. "Marcas wants what I want." I affirm, passing her into the kitchen.

"Wise man." Jamie smirks, following me. "So, you think he's ready for this?"

"I know he's not. He thinks he is, but, well, you know my mom."

"Take pictures! Better yet, video!" Jamie laughs. "Especially when your mom sinks her teeth into him."

I laugh, knowing no one can meet Fae Donnelly and leave unscathed by her quirky and sometimes blush-worthy interactions.

"By the way, we missed the end of July car show today," Jamie says with a frown. "Slipped my mind completely."

"I remember, but I didn't feel like going. Crowded streets and all the fuss. Didn't sound too appealing to me."

"Yeah, not sure I'd have gone either if I'd remembered."

The front door slowly opens. Marcas' gorgeous green eyes gleam at us as he steps inside. "You about ready?"

"Almost," I say, turning to Jamie. A broad, impish grin greets me. Ignoring it, I ask, "Is Finn coming over soon?"

She nods. "Thanks again for letting us use your kitchen. He just loves cooking in your pans."

"Glad I could help. We'll be back later. Not sure when, though."

"You two lovebirds, have fun! I hope it's not too scary for ya!" Jamie adds as I walk to Marcas.

"He'll do fine. Nothing to worry about." I smile warmly at him. "Just no sudden movements." Then I wink.

Jamie and I laugh when Marcas' smile falters.

Though the sky is blue and clear, and the breeze is light, we decide to drive. As we pull up to my parent's house, butterflies flutter around in my insides. Why am I so nervous?

"Wow, their yard is huge! Look at those trees," Marcas muses as we get out of the car and walk through the white archway threshold of my parent's yard.

"They're my favorite too." When I grab Marcas' hand, it is cold and damp with sweat. "You doing all right, Marcas?"

"Mhmm." He gives a stiff smile, his jaw firm.

We continue down the sidewalk to the front door and then stop. "This is great—gonna be great," I say, though I don't know who needs to be reassured more, him or me? Slowly, I reach my hand up to the door, but Marcas grabs it before I have a chance to knock.

"You're sure you want to do this right now. We could wait a bit."

"Are you kidding? You practically begged me for this!"

Marcas shakes his head. "I don't—I don't recall wanting—not right now."

"Oh really?" I suppress a laugh. "Hmm, I seem to recall your exact words were, 'Most definitely'. Were they not?"

He shrugs and looks away, hiding his smile.

"Huh, so what happened to the Marcas who's not afraid of anything?"

Sweat glistens on his brow when he turns back to me. He dabs it away with the back of his hand. "Well, he's never had to meet someone's parents before, now, has he?"

"If I didn't know any better, I'd say you're more afraid of them than you ever were of Conall." I laugh when his lip snarls.

"So, we'll leave," I say, turning around.

He tugs my arm around behind me and pulls me close. "We will do no such thing." His dimpled smile draws me into a kiss. Then he gazes into my eyes, his seductive sea of green making me not only weak in the knees but temporarily forget the dilemma we face.

Breathless I suggest, "We could call, say we won't make it?"

"I'm ready . . . I just need a minute more." Then he kisses me again. If he keeps that up, I'll need a lot more than a minute to recover. "One more time, remind me why we're doing this?" He whispers at my neck just under my ear. A tingling spark of energy zings its way down my side.

"Be-because Judy . . . can't keep her mouth shut." I say winded.

"Right, entirely her fault. Got it!" He whispers again, his lips caressing my earlobe. "But you could've denied it. I mean. . ."

Reality rattles me out of his trance. Shaking my thoughts clear, I untangle myself from him and straighten my disheveled clothes. "Well, my mom didn't give me a chance now, did she? Fell right into her trap. Confirm my plans, then tell me to bring you—brilliant!" I mumble.

Laughing, he takes my hand again and squeezes.

Breathing in through my nose, I blow it out through my mouth, and try to steady my beating heart. "Let's just get through this. You'll meet, they'll love you and then we're outta here."

"Shae?"

When I look at him, I see nothing but love and support smiling back at me.

"Here we go," I say, then knock on the door.

Muffled yelps come through the crack under the door, followed by loud sniffs trailing back and forth.

"Stop that. Go on, Mr. Darcy, get out of the way," my mom says, and then opens the door a crack. Tiny barks erupt from a fluffy, flat-faced snowball of a puppy at her feet.

"You got a dog?" I ask as she opens the door wider. The rat-like critter runs to Marcas, yelping and nipping at his feet.

"Hey, you made it!" Mom says, fully extending the door open and stepping outside. "And who's this handsome young man?"

"This is Marcas, Mom. Marcas, my mom, Fae."

"Don't you just look all tall, dark, and handsome? Sorry, I just need to—" She tugs him close and gently wraps her arms around him as she rests her head on his upper shoulder. "Dreamy!" She sighs.

Suppressing a laugh, I watch Marcas stiffen as if trapped, soon to be eaten alive, yet ready to bold the first chance he gets.

"It's a . . . pleasure to meet you, ma'am," he says when she backs up to get another good look at him.

"How sweet you are! Well, we're just so excited you could make it on such short notice."

"Yeah, it's like it's meant to be," I say with a smile, though my sarcasm is thick enough that even she can't mistake it.

"Indeed." She pulls me in for a hug. "He's so charming, Shae. Great job!" she whispers loudly, sending my cheeks ablaze. She then winks at us both

156

before stepping closer to Marcas. The mischievous look in her eyes makes my stomach flop.

"Gosh, I'm just so happy you two are here!" She puts her hands on Marcas' cheeks and pulls him in, smacking a kiss to the right of his unsuspecting lips. "Such a delight!" Then she releases him, grabs his hand and heads to the door without giving a second thought to just how outrageous her gesture had been. "Come inside. Make yourself at home."

Marcas, being pulled along by my mother into the house, looks back at me with perplexity in his eyes as the yapping dog scurries past. I snicker and shrug as I follow. If the boys were to ever hear about this, they would never let him live it down.

The smell of fire-grilled chicken fills the house as we move down the hall to the kitchen.

"I hope you came hungry, Marcas, because we've got plenty!"

Marcas smiles warmly at her. "Yes, ma'am. It smells wonderful. I can't wait."

"No! Mr. Darcy, enough barking. Go on. To bed!" The dog barks once more, then scampers off into the other room, its little claws scraping on the linoleum floor.

Mother moves to the sink and starts chopping tomatoes. "You have family in town, Marcas?"

Leaning against the door frame, Marcas looks at me for a fraction of a second, but it's enough for me to see his nerves kicking in again. I can only imagine how difficult it is to talk about the loss of a parent, let alone both.

"Other than my brothers, a cousin. But she left just this morning."

"And your parents? Where are they?"

"They're both gone, ma'am."

She stops cutting and turns around. "Both? Goodness, you poor boys. That's it. You come over anytime you need a good home-cooked meal. Bring your brothers."

"We couldn't imp—"

"Nope, I insist. Anytime. In fact, we'll set something up before you leave." She winks.

"Well, thank you." Then he glances at me and smiles.

Eagerness bubbles to life inside me. I almost feel bad for subjecting him to Mom's quirky behavior test, but if he wants to be with me, I need to know he accepts all parts of me—cooky parents and all.

Picking up the cutting board, Mom scrapes the tomatoes off into a small glass bowl with her knife. "I think we're about finished here. Dale's out back flipping the chicken on the grill, Marcas," she says, pointing to the back door with her knife. "You're welcome to join him while Shae and I bring out the rest of the food."

Marcas straightens up, "All right," but he doesn't move.

I go take his arm and guide him to the back door. "I'll be out in a sec, I promise. You'll do fine."

Hesitant, Marcas steps out. The screen door automatically slams closed as I walk back to the sink.

"Shae, I think you've found a keeper!"

My cheeks redden to what I assume is the bright color of the tomato she is currently cutting. "Mom, you've only just met him."

"Well, as far as first impressions go, he did right by me. He-he's great, Shae, really."

"Hah, and you know that how?"

She shrugs. "A mother just knows. Like the way he looks at you. How he holds himself. Nope. No warnings, no secrets hidden there."

I almost laugh aloud. "I'm glad you approve." Part of the fear clinging to every fiber of my being melts away. She approves. But will she still when she knows our secret?

"How did he ask you out? Was it romantic?" She swoons, resting her head on my shoulder.

"You mean Judy didn't tell you?"

Mom frowns and goes back to cutting. "Don't fault her for caring."

"Is that what you call it?"

"I would! She was downright distraught when she heard . . . Well, anyway, she hoped you'd find someone better soon. And look, you did! Found the perfect guy."

Pressing my lips together, I force a smile. The fact is, if Judy had kept her gossipy mouth shut, we wouldn't be in this predicament.

"Hardly call it perfect, Mom. It was a mess at first. More complicated than anything."

"Well, that's okay too. Some of the best love stories start with a good chase."

"Uh, Mom, let's not get ahead of ourselves. We're taking things slow, making sure we're a good fit."

"Not too slow, I hope. We don't want this one getting away!"

Gulping down her heavy meaning, I try to stifle the exact fear that's been front and center in my mind for so long that I may implode from it. "I don't intend to."

Seeing my melancholy, she pulls me into a hug. "No, no, of course you don't!" Stepping back, she puts her hands on my forearms. "Please don't mistake my enthusiasm for recklessness. I just don't want to see you holding back out of fear. Every second counts. When you know—"

"Why wait?" we say in unison.

She grins warmly and caresses my cheek. "Exactly."

Fancy that, something Marcas and my mother have in common—the need to press forward with love, letting nothing stand in your way.

"But we are, though, Mom—taking it slow. For now, at least. We've decided."

"Okay, fine." She shrugs and starts putting dirty dishes in the sink. "I won't say anything more about it. Except that early fall is a wonderful time for a wedding—just putting that out there," she adds, grabbing the glass bowl and platter of finger foods off the counter next to her.

"Mom."

"Be a dear and grab the utensils and napkins." She motions with her head for me to follow out the back door.

"Mom!" I whisper harshly, but she continues to walk with a happy bounce to the door.

As we exit the house, we see Marcas, leaning against the garage frame with a drink in hand, laughing robustly along with my father by the grill, wearing his usual red-striped chef's apron.

Mom and I slowly set our items on the picnic table.

"What's going on out here?" I ask, eyeing my dad, then Marcas.

Marcas' grin grows, sending a warning tingling down my spine.

"Dad," I say, walking over to him and wrapping my arms around him.

"Pumpkin." He hugs me uncharacteristically tight. It makes me not only gasp for breath but also question his motives. He releases me, and I glimpse a glisten in his eyes before he turns to my mother.

"You two, sit and relax. Oh, and there's drinks in the cooler," Mom says, shushing Dad toward the house. "We'll get the rest," she adds just before the door slams closed.

"What are they playing at?" I say, keeping my eyes on the door.

Marcas puts his drink down on the table behind me and pulls me close. Automatically, I place my hand on his hips but remain distracted by the noises from inside.

He turns my chin to face him. "So, how'd it go?"

"Oh, she knows. I don't know how, but she does. I'd swear to it." Taking a celery stick, I dip it in the ranch and then crunch down on it aggressively. As I chew, I narrow my eyes on Marcas and his extensively wide, knowing smile. "What were you two laughing about?"

His smile holds an unfamiliar glimmer of mischievousness, making his eyes sparkle and exposing his hidden dimples that always melt my butter. He bites into a crisp baby carrot and chews smugly.

"What? What'd I miss? Why are you laughing?"

"Your father. He's actually quite funny."

"Hah! No, he's not."

Marcas shrugs. "Seemed to be to me."

Distrusting his coyness, I raise my eyebrow to a point and eye him harder.

Marcas pulls me closer and looks seductively into my eyes. "You're sexy when you're interrogating, you know that?"

"Don't distract me with your sweet-talk. I wanna know!"

"Hmm. What can I say? I'm just an easy guy to get along with." When my scowl deepens, he laughs. "Why so surprised? He can't be that tough a guy, he liked Jared, didn't he?"

The sudden mention of his name on Marcas' lips throws me. Swallowing down the discomfort, I clear my throat. "I wouldn't go as far as to say that."

"Oh, I just assumed—" Marcas grows silent.

When I try to pull away, Marcas holds me firm in place, as if he knows I want to run as far from this conversation as I can. I don't want him to know this part of my past. To have such an embarrassing secret revealed makes me feel weak, and pathetically young and naïve. But if we are to move forward together, I know I need to release what I've clung to for far too long.

"Jared was a charmer," I say somberly after taking a long moment to collect my words. "He could change your mind with a smile. My parents felt that something was off about him, but I didn't want to listen. I was desperate for someone to see me, you know. Just once, notice something in me worth loving."

Marcas grabs my hands and holds them tight. The doleful look in his eyes makes my chest tighten, forcing me to look away.

"I followed him to Seattle. Pathetic, I know. I'd only known him for a couple of months. But, like I said, charming. But also, manipulative. Though I didn't see it at the time. He convinced me I was being paranoid. Then he started restricting what I could do, where I could go, and who I could see, to the point that I hardly left the house except for when I went school and for groceries.

And those who knew never said a word. Not even when we were about to walk down the aisle. I was so humiliated, standing there waiting for him, only to find out he wasn't coming, and why."

My heart aches to reveal such a horrible memory, but I do not cry. There are no tears left in me for what he's done. Looking up, I see Marcas' sad eyes staring back, and the weight of the dark secret I've carried for so long leaves me. "You have to know, Marcas, there's no love in me for him anymore. But the fear is still there. Will my parents like you? Will my father approve, and when the time comes, give his consent? Or will I have to walk away from them for the man I love?"

"Shhh, Shae. I would never—"

"I would! In a heartbeat, because I don't doubt us. Not this time. I know you're a good man, Marcas—different from anyone I've ever met. But we both know people talk."

Lowering his head, Marcas mumbles, "Duke's."

"If they knew about us, then they'd have to know about that. I don't want—I couldn't handle it if they—"

Marcas pulls me into a tight hug. I want to get lost in it. Forget where we are and why we're here, but I know my parents will come back out eventually.

"No one should ever have to go through something like that. You're so very strong."

I smile a little, though he can't see it. "Either that, or incredibly naïve and gullible."

"No, Shae, he was selfish and took advantage of you—lied and betrayed your trust. He chose to cheat rather than end it. No part of that is on you."

"Okay, well, maybe you're right, but what if my parents don't approve of you either?"

"I don't know; your mom seemed to think highly of me. She did kiss me, you know." I can feel his body shaking as he chuckles.

"True!" I say, looking up at him and smiling. "And you took it like a champ."

His features falter. "She does that to everyone, doesn't she?"

"But she seemed to fancy you more." My grin broadens.

"All right then, see, nothing to worry about. We've got this. You and me."

"That's right! It *is* about us, not him or them or—"

"Exactly." His eyes shimmer as he smiles with a knowing grin.

Tingles of warning tumble wildly in my stomach. "Dang it! You distracted me. Tell me right now!"

Marcas laughs boisterously. "All right, all right, you were right. He's pretty intimidating."

"See! Okay so what happened?"

"I came out, shook his hand firmly, so he knew I meant it, and introduced myself. It was good." Marcas grabs his cup off the table and takes a drink. "Of course he had questions. I answered, and we talked some more. You were inside for a while. I don't know, it just felt like the right moment—for there to be no confusion about my intentions. He looked me straight in the eyes—I thought he was going to punch me—but then he slapped his hand on my shoulder, put a drink in my hand, and said, *'All right then.'*"

"Wait, what?"

"Yeah, I think he likes me. Even invited me to go fishing!" Marcas says matter-of-factly and takes another drink.

"Wh-wait, I'm confused. What felt right?" My body stiffens. "Intentions?" I gasp.

"I'm sorry, I know we agreed, but—"

"But-but Marcas, the plan? I-I—"

"Please don't be upset. I—"

Shaking my head fervently, I then eye Marcas as I jerk the drink out of his hands and gulp the rest down in one swallow, then cringe at its flavor. Then I put the cup down on the table with a heavy thud.

"Are you mad?"

"Yes, I'm mad! We had a plan, Marcas."

"I know, I'm sorry, I shouldn't have asked without you here"

Without me? My stomach drops as if coming off a steep drop. This isn't just about my future, it's his too. If he had been a regular boy asking a regular girl's father for her hand, would she be there? No. Finding out he had asked, would she be this upset to learn of it? Again, no. Quite the opposite, actually.

"Answer me one thing, Marcas," I say, looking firmly in his eyes. "Did you plan to do this all along?"

"No," he says, his deep, serious tone carrying with it regret. "It just felt right."

Now how can I be mad at that? Spontaneous conviction only a true leader can possess. It's one of the many things I love about him.

Nodding, I say, "Okay, well, you better brace yourself then."

"What? Why? It can't be that ba—"

High-pitched girlish screams come from inside the house, growing louder when the back door violently swings open, slamming against the house.

"Wanna bet?" I mumble.

"I can't believe you didn't tell me!" Mom squeals, darting across the yard toward us with arms outstretched. "All that time and not a word!"

Marcas tries to back away, but I hold him tight. No way I'm dealing with this alone.

Pummeling into us, Mom grabs us both in a hug and jumps us up and down. "I practically had to beat it out of your father. *Ahhh!* This is so exciting! My baby is getting married!"

'You asked for it,' I mouth to Marcas as we bob all over the place.

'I love you,' Marcas mouths back and smiles.

CHAPTER 12

Let The Planning Begin

At first, it comes as a distant thudding—a rap, rap, rapping, so quiet, so far away, I cannot tell if the knocking at the front door is real or part of my dream. Trying to ignore it, I tuck the blankets around my ears. But as my consciousness evolves, the pounding persistently intensifies. More asleep than awake, I fumble blindly for my phone on the nightstand next to the bed, and then squint from the bright screen when it turns on. It takes a second for the numbers seven and twenty-five to come into focus on the screen.

Ugh, "It's too early!" I groan loudly as if whoever is at the door will not only hear me but also knock off the insistent berating of my door and go away because I'm not getting out of this warm bed for anybody.

Tax lets out a muffled, snorted bark as he stands by the closed bedroom door.

"Shae, open up! It's Mom." Her voice carries through the house like a gunshot.

Bolting upright in bed, I scramble to my feet, grab my robe from the chair and wrap it around me as I open the bedroom door. Tax takes off for the front door and I follow, grumbling, "She had better not be here for—"

"Oh, good, you are awake!" she says, coming inside the second the door opens. Three weighted bags hang from her forearms. "Didn't you hear me knocking?"

As I rub the sleep from my eyes, I smile sardonically. "Oh, I heard."

"Then what took so long?" She grins at me, then her lips droop. "You know, you really shouldn't sleep with your makeup on. I hear it causes premature aging."

"Mom, wh-what are you doing—did you need something?"

"I just thought I'd stop by," she says, setting the bags on the coffee table with a weighted thud. "I did some light reading last night and thought I'd share!"

"Uh, light?" My eyes widen as she pulls stacks of magazines out of the bags and puts them on the table.

"I didn't go through all of them." She grins, sitting down on the long couch by the window. "I thought we could together."

But it's not even 8 am! "Now?" I say, slowly sitting on the arm of the loveseat.

"It's just—" She shakes her head and gently dabs a glistening tear out of the corner of her eye with tissue from her pocket. "My baby."

"Mom, stop. I'm only getting married," I say flatly, though I struggle to get the words out myself. It sounds so surreal. Married. I almost don't believe it's actually happening.

"So very happy." She grins at me through her tears. "And you know." She sniffs. "It's not every day your one and only daughter gets married."

The look of utter happiness shining through her teary, red, bloodshot eyes gives me pause. How can I blame her for acting this way? She's wanted this for me for so long. To expect her to behave any differently is just plain unrealistic.

"How did you even—you only found out two days ago? When did you even have time to get all these?"

She glances at the table, then back at me, the corners of her lips turned up. "I may or may not have been grabbing a few here and there while I've been out."

Her sheepish smirk almost makes me give in to her insanity. But sleep still has a hold on me. "Look, I want to do this with you. I do, but—"

"It's early, I know." She sniffles and wipes her eyes. "Your dad and I are just so excited for you."

"I know. But not before nine, okay?"

She shakes her head fervently then nods. "Of course. I'll be better."

"Why don't you—" I am about to offer to have her stay while I get ready, but as I watch her eyeball the dirty dishes in my sink, I think better of it. "—head to Celie's and save us a table? I'll meet you there in about twenty minutes or so. Okay?"

"Breakfast and planning. I like it!" she says happily, then shoves the magazines back into her bags. "You want me to order you something?"

"Eggs," I say, walking her to the door. When I open it, she steps outside. "And hashbrowns and a side of pancakes."

She cringes, which I try to ignore.

"Carbs? You sure? You have a wedding dress to fit into, you know?"

"Bye, Mom," I say, then smile and wave as the door closes.

*   *   *

With my head slightly tilted, I squint my eyes fervently. "Mom, I can't—am I supposed to see a difference?"

She taps her pointy finger on the magazine page. "See the tiny roses bordering the plates? And the daisies on this one? The cups are wider at the base here too." A slight smile forms on her face as she pats my hand on the table. "Honestly, Shae, you need to snap out of it. We've been at this for over a week and still have so much more to decide on."

Looking at the pictures again, I sigh and bite my lower lip. It's no use. I just don't care about all this fancy stuff! "What are these even for?"

"It'll be for the cake you and Marcas share."

With a pressed smile on my face and my eyebrows raised, I shrug my shoulders. "The daisies?"

"See, not so hard, now, is it?" She then bends the corner of the page and puts the magazine on the medium-sized sack to her left.

Watching my mom like a ball of energy, I recall the last time we planned a wedding together. Or, I should say, didn't. My last engagement was anything but a cause for celebration for my parents—my mother in particular. At first, she was hesitant to even speak of it, let alone accept it as reality. It didn't help

173

that Jared's rich parents took over everything, insisting we use their wedding coordinator. It had left little else for my mother and me to do together, that is, when she had finally warmed up to the idea, which was about a degree above freezing. Regardless, I knew it had hurt her deeply to be left out, though she refused to let it show.

At least when the wedding was called off, Jared's parents were left to pay the bill and not mine. As was rightly so since it was their son who left me to run off to marry his mistress. Nonetheless, it stung to have such an *I told you so* from my mom hanging over my head as I dealt with all the feels that had come with such a rejection. She never actually said it aloud to me, though, but I knew she had to have been thinking it.

A shudder flickers in my body, the residual heartache and pain of that moment momentarily surfacing—hopefully for the very last time.

Seeing my mother gleam as she jots down notes in our wedding binder, I feel hard knots begin to twist in my stomach. Secrets tear people apart, and I'm keeping the biggest one from them. Will they ever forgive me?

Judy, our server, who has been slowly leaning in, peers over us while refilling a water glass. "Daisies—always a good choice," she whispers and nudges my shoulder with her elbow.

"Why, thank you, Judy." Mom smiles.

"How's all the weddin' prep comin'? I sure do luv when you two come in carrian on about all this. Brightens up my day!" Judy puts one cup down and fills the other. Distracted by all the wedding mess, she spills a little over the side onto the floor. "And I just knew you two were meant to be." She winks at me, a grin on her face.

I give her a sardonic grin back. Yeah, you knew enough to spread it all through town!

Mom nudges my arm. "Well, if I can get this one to focus, maybe we'll finish in time."

"Ha-ha," I say, tossing a magazine toward her. She stops it in mid-slide with the slap of her hand on the table, then opens it and starts skimming the pages like she had asked for it.

"Well, I'll leave you to it. Let me know if you need anythin'." Judy steps away to another table.

"Speaking of Marcas, wasn't he coming today?" Mom asks, then licks her fingers before turning the page.

Pretending to be interested in an article about *'Up-dos or down-dos? What's best for your big day?'* I give a pause, then casually turn a page. "He, uh, said if he could get away, then maybe."

"For heaven's sake, he's only 24. What could he possibly be doing to keep so busy?"

"Beats me. Work, I guess," I say, glancing at the large clock on the wall. "*Six*! Already? Shoot, I promised Jamie I'd meet at the cabin, and it's a mess."

"Busy girl. Well, give her loves for me then."

"Thanks again for the help today, Mom," I say as I scramble to retrieve my things. "You're a lifesaver!"

"You remember that the next time you complain about having to make so many decisions."

"You know you love to torture me."

"On the contrary! All are very necessary." She smirks though she tries to keep a straight face.

"Right, and whose house looks like a bridal boutique again?"

"Aw, but the imageboard. You doubted it, but it works!"

"As what? A weapon? Dad's poor head."

"I warned him not to leave his shoes near the tripod."

We both laugh as we gather the rest of our stuff.

Stuck between some magazines, a small envelope flutters to the floor.

"Shoot!" I say, retrieving it from the floor and handing it to her. "Sorry, Mom. It was taped to your front door earlier when I was there grabbing the stuff you asked for."

"Hmm." Taking it from me, she slowly flips it over. The back is as blank as the front. Slipping the piece of paper out, she unfolds it. "Wonder who it could be—" Her eyes move rapidly, back and forth, as she reads. The more her eyes travel the page, the more firm her pressed lips become. With her brow furrowed, she then folds the paper, creasing the edges tightly, and stuffs it in her bag.

"Mom, what is it?"

She continues to gather her things.

"Mom?"

"Hmm, what, dear?" she asks, looking scatterbrained at me.

"The envelope?"

"Oh, um . . . nothing." She smiles, though her eyes hold a hint of worry. "Just a reminder that I'd promised to do something for someone." She caresses her soft hand under my chin. "Shae, really, it's nothing. Now you'd better get going. You don't wanna keep Jamie waiting."

"Dang it! Your house tomorrow, right?" I say in a rush. "Same time?"

Stacking the rest of our mess, she nods.

"Jamie's coming. I figured we could use her creative juices." When Mom doesn't respond, I touch her back gently while she grabs her purse from the back of the chair. "Mom?"

"What?" She looked at me and then around, disoriented.

I breathe out hard, pick up her keys off the table, and hand them over. "Nothing. See you tomorrow."

She hugs me tight, then walks to the counter to pay the bill.

Out on the sidewalk, we wave goodbye before going our separate ways.

Though she said it was nothing, a sinking feeling weighs heavily in my gut. I haven't seen her this out of sorts since she learned of her father's passing when I was sixteen. But if it was truly nothing, why hesitate to give me a look-see? I wish I had just read it when I had the chance. Now it will torment my curiosity to no end.

To get to my to-do list, I hustle down the street. When I pass the antique store with the tall, scantily dressed, creepy, headless mannequin in the window, my phone buzzes, Marcas' face covering the screen.

"Hey, you missed the seating charts today."

"Ah, man, I was really looking forward to that, too!" Marcas says in a playful tone.

"It was riveting. Truly. Having the proper family member-to-friend ratio is no laughing matter. Just ask my mom."

"You get done what you needed?"

"I guess so. I keep having this dream where I'm walking down the street and people start throwing bouquets of flowers at me, screaming, *Colors matter. Pick one!*"

He laughs again. "You think we can pull this off? Two weddings in a little over two weeks? Seems unnecessary. Can't we just tell your—"

"No!" I say firmly. "What if they freak—think you're some kind of delusional crazy person? I can't—I won't let them—" Breathing heavily, I inhale and hold it in. Marcas remains silent on the other end. "We agreed, Marcas. Not until after."

For a moment longer, the line is quiet. Too quiet.

"All right," he finally says, a hint of frustration lingering in his tone. "If that's what you want."

No, it's not what I want! I want the magic—the natural, authentic emotions that come when two people join together forever in front of the ones they love. Is that too much to ask? Not some rehearsal wedding for my parent's sake because they have no idea what Marcas is or what world I'm about to be a part of. It breaks my heart to lie to them, but it's what has to be done right now. I can't risk everything by telling them. I will not be forced to choose between Marcas and them. I won't do it!

"Did you find a place, then?" I say, trying not to sound like the frustrated bride-to-be inside my head.

"Sam did, not too far from the clearing where we—where you were when—"

"Conall attacked me?"

"Mhmm. There are flowers growing in a circle. Sam says the arch will fit there perfectly."

"Really?" I say as I walk up to the candy store and pause. "Who knew Sam was such a softy?"

"They're building part of the arch now. But we can change the location if it's too—"

"No, it'll be perfect." Though that pivotal location was the start of my troubles, it was also where I first saw Marcas in his inherent form. Protector, provider, and wolf devoted to my heart. "Just perfect."

"I have news about Conall."

I swallow hard, my twitterpated excitement dissipating in a puff of bitter smoke.

"Korin's men spotted some of Conall's followers leaving Nebraska a day ago in a pack of seven."

"We're never going to find him."

"He can't hide forever."

"Did Korin find out—?"

"No sign of Ardan either."

"What about Vevina? Is she still not talking?"

Marcas exhaled forcefully. "I don't think she'll ever turn on Conall."

"How can she stay loyal to that lunatic after the way he treated her? I wouldn't stand for it."

"She's been brainwashed into submission, Shae. Hardwired to be faithful till the end. Tynan has a few tactics he's trying to break through, but I don't know."

"I'm so sorry, Marcas. Don't give up. She's your sister; you never know."

Marcas hasn't come right out and said it, but I know it torments him severely, knowing she's been alive all these years, partnered with his enemy. Even still, after Conall abandoned her, she stayed loyal. It's heartbreaking.

"Marcas."

"Mo Chroi."

The use of his usual pet name for me brings a smile to my lips. "Will I see you tonight?"

"I'd like that. But we still have so much to do. I'll stop by later if I can."

"You know where I'll be."

I stuff the phone in my pocket and open the door to the shop. Upon entry, I am not only hit with the overwhelming sweet and delicious smells of berries but also by a portly, gray-haired older woman with sharp elbows, being escorted on the arm by a tall, young man.

"Watch where ye be," the woman grumbles in a gruff Irish accent as she watches me keenly with her cold grayish blue eyes.

"I'm sorry, I didn't—"

"Pay her no mind, ma'am," the young man says with a slight accent himself. He tips his head full of light, wavy red hair at me while holding the door open. His eyes, bright as the bluest of skies, sparkle as he smiles. A spray of light colored freckles rest on his nose and cheeks.

When I move past him and into the store, the amulet under my shirt subtly vibrates, like the pulsating heartbeat of a fluttering hummingbird. But as quickly as it started, it stopped. And if it weren't for the fact that I've only felt such a prompting around only two other people, and neither one is close by, I wouldn't give it a second thought. But something tells me it isn't as innocent as a fluke. Marcas did say others were bound to come looking. Could this stranger be one of them?

The door closes with a ring-a-ding of the bell on the handle behind me, bringing me out of my thoughts. Moving about, I gather an array of sweet treats for later, then head home.

Right when I reach the cabin, Jamie joins me, coming in the opposite direction.

"You're just getting here?" Jamie grabs the gate since my hands are full. The gravel under our feet crunches loudly as we move to the other side.

"Yeah, I had a few things to get for tonight."

Watching me struggle with the key, she takes it from me and unlocks the front door. Dense, warm air rushes at us as the door swings open wide. We leave it that way as we move to the living room.

"I couldn't decide, so I got all the good stuff." I grin and dump the bags on the small couch just inside the door.

"Oooh, lemme take a look see!" She rushes over and rifles through them, mumbling under her breath, "Where's the chocolate?"

"Have you heard from Finn today?" I ask, knowing chocolate is her go-to stress reliever.

"Huh, for like two seconds. No thanks to your fiancé. He screamed at him to get back to work."

I walk to the window and unlock it. "Marcas doesn't scream," I grunt, lifting it open, and then I proceed to the other one. Cool, refreshing air rushes in, instantly taking the edge off.

Jamie looks at me, her eyebrow peaked.

"Yeah, well, you prepare two weddings at once and see how you'd be."

"Uh, try one, and he's not doing it alone!" Jamie scoffs, plopping on the long couch by the window, her hand full of chocolate morsels. She pops one into her mouth as the wind ruffles her hair across her shoulders and face.

"Okay, so he's stressed. Can you blame him?" I say, moving the bags over so I can sit. "I mean, I don't know the first thing about planning a midnight wolf wedding. Do you?"

"All right, fine, but could you at least ask him to lighten up? I miss my boyfriend!"

As I empty the contents of each bag onto the table in front of me, a nagging feeling takes over as I recall Marcas and our earlier conversation.

"Did Finn tell you about Conall when you talked?"

Jamie's body tenses slightly, and what's left of her somewhat lighthearted smile fades when she looks at me and nods.

No matter how much Jamie denies having any lasting angst from what happened to her, I know something's changed. Fear never seemed to faze her before, but now I see glimpses of it in her eyes from time to time.

"I can't wait for this double wedding nightmare to be over," she mumbles.

"Gee, thanks a lot!"

"You know what I mean." Though she smiles, her body remains stiff. "The constant looking over our shoulders, wondering when he'll show up again. Kind of over it."

"Trust me, August 23rd can't come soon enough."

As she watches me, her grimace morphs into a smile, and she laughs. "Okay, fine, whatever. Have you picked out a dress yet?"

"No." I sigh as I get up and go into the kitchen to toss the bags in a reusable bin. "They're all so—"

"Expensive?"

"Revealing."

"Excuse me! Strapless, empire-waisted gowns are *not* revealing. They're classy and elegant," she says, putting her feet on the coffee table.

"Maybe on you. I look like a kid playing dress-up."

Pulling the fridge door open, I see nothing but an almost empty jar of pickles, a couple of half-eaten slices of sample wedding cake left over from the taste testing we did a few days ago, an apple, and four cans of soda.

"You better pick something soon," Jamie calls louder.

Something to eat or my dress? At this point, they both seem like a lost cause.

"I have one of um. Mom helped pick it. It should be here soon." Slamming the fridge closed, I move to the cupboard, finding a box of mac and cheese, saltine crackers, and a can of spam I don't even recall buying. Why did I not buy something other than candy and junk food while out?

Returning to the fridge, I grab two sodas and then head back into the living room and sit with an umph on the loveseat. The cool air in the room at least comforts me when food won't.

"You know, I've been thinking about what dress to get for the forest wedding, and I'm not sure I want a traditional one. Seems out of place to be so dressed up."

"Ugh, not a plain churchy dress, *please!*" she says, rolling her eyes as she strings her fingers through her hair.

"Nothing like that. Just something to represent the big change I'm about to go through." Reaching over, I hand her one of the sodas, then I sink back into the cushions and exhale the heavy load weighing on my mind.

She taps the top of her can. "I like that—a dress to fit your change."

"Whatever that'll look like." My shoes fall to the ground as I slip them off and put my feet up. Soda mist sprays from our cans as we simultaneously open them.

"It's a good thing you don't have a sucky maid-of-honor without fashion connections in New York and LA!" She grins and takes a drink.

"A cousin interning at Bloomingdales hardly passes as having fashion cred."

Jamie kicks her foot at me playfully. "Yeah, well, that's more connections than you have at the moment. Besides, he knows people. I'll have him ask around."

"Why bother? I can't afford anything custom-made anyway."

"Didn't Marcas say he'd take care of it?"

"I can't—it's too much."

"Shae, you're going to be a queen. What says that more than a Maggie Sottero or a Vera Wang original?"

She's right. If I am to be a queen, shouldn't I look it? But to spend that much on a one-time dress seems wasteful, even if it is fit for royalty.

"I'll think about it."

"You gonna think about telling your parents what Marcas and his brothers are while you're at it?"

I frown. "When? Huh? How? It's not like that kind of stuff comes up at family get-togethers. *'Hey Mom, Dad, guess what? Marcas and his brothers are shape-shifting wolves. Pretty crazy, huh? Oh, and by the way, we need to have the wedding at midnight so I can become a wolf too—and also their new queen. Could you pass the peas, please?'*"

Jamie sputters, trying not to spew soda all over the couch.

I laugh too; Jamie's reaction is too funny to hold back.

"Seriously though, Jamie. How?"

"Girl, I don't know. You guys are close. I'm sure your mom will understand. At least a hell of a lot better than my parents would."

"You sure about that? An amulet predicting my fate? Sounds a bit far-fetched."

"You believed it."

"Yeah, well, I had a vision. It's kind of hard to deny what I've seen with my own eyes. She'll think I'm naïve or an idiot for believing in fairytales and folklore."

"Or she'll think it's badass like we do! Look, she already likes him—thinks he's perfect. Practically takes credit for the two of you, even. I doubt she'll lose

187

her mind. I'm not saying she won't freak a bit at first—it's only natural—but still."

I chuckle lightly. Jamie's right. Mom couldn't love Marcas more than if she'd hand-picked him herself. But would she still feel that way when she knew their secret?

"But what if she thinks Marcas is insane, making the whole thing up—makes me call off the wedding because of it?"

"I really don't know, Shae. You'll just have to trust that she loves you enough not to make you choose. He makes you happy. Anyone can see that. She won't be rash. She'll listen. I know she will."

"They keep asking where Marcas is whenever I go over, and I hate lying to them."

"You might want to figure it out soon—just sayin'."

She's right, but I still have no resolution on how to make it happen.

We sit for a few minutes, the room getting cooler by the minute and the yard outside getting darker.

A big gust of wind rushes through the open window, swirling around the room. The front door jerks shut with a heavy slam, making us both scream. Then we laugh profusely.

"So, what'll it be? Pizza or Mexican?" I ask, throwing a fluffy pillow. It hits Jamie in the face, making her hair flop up.

Clutching the pillow with her hands, she slowly lowers it. An oversized, mischievous grin shines on her face.

"Both," we say together, and then laugh. Then she chucks the pillow back at me. It whizzes over my head and lands in the middle of the kitchen floor.

CHAPTER 13

A Moment Of Silence

Three-fourths of a medium pepperoni pizza sit untouched in the box on the coffee table with a half eaten burrito and a mound of soggy nachos in white styrofoam takeout containers beside it.

The only light in the room comes from the television in the corner, flickering on the walls like sluggish strobe lights.

Jamie, asleep on the couch, has her legs across my lap. She crashed about thirty minutes into the movie, but I didn't bother waking her. She had just as long of a day as I did.

Tired but not sleepy, I check the clock on the wall. 11:47 pm. It says the same on my phone. No text messages or missed calls, though.

Inhaling through my nostrils, I then exhale through pursed lips and blink twice to refocus my eyes on the TV screen.

A quiet double tap sounds at the window behind my head, making a cold rush shoot through my body. The taps happen again, making Jamie curl her legs up and roll over, pulling the blanket over her shoulder.

The front door slowly opens with a soft, subtle creak. Marcas pops his head in, smiling, his big green eyes staring back at me. "You awake?"

"No. Couldn't you hear me snoring?"

"You sure that's not Jamie?" He chuckles quietly as he comes into the house and takes his shoes off at the door. He then walks across the room, leans over Jamie, places his soft, sweet lips on mine, and then steps back and collapses on the loveseat behind him. Dark circles line under his eyes.

"You hungry? There's pizza," I whisper.

"Starving," he says, though he doesn't move.

"That tired, huh?"

He exhales long and hard. "No more than you, I'm sure."

"We're all a bunch of fuddy-duddies."

"Yeah, well." Stretching back, his arms over his head, he pops his back and grunts. "There's nothing like a full day's work to help you sleep." Then he reaches over and snags a slice of pizza, biting into it as he sits back.

"Sorry, the wedding stuff is so time-consuming."

"But worth it." He pats the couch cushion next to him and grins a large, sweet smile. Without hesitation, I go to his side. He wraps his arm around me, and I snuggle against his warm chest.

"You look exhausted," he says with a mouth full of pizza.

"Back at ya, Sweetheart." I smile, though he can't see it at this angle. "It's a new look. You like? I call it frazzled bride!"

Instead of laughing, he sighs. "Maybe I shouldn't stay long."

"No! Stay, *please!*" I wrap my arms around his midsection and squeeze.

"Ooh!" Marcas inhales sharply. "Shae, be careful there."

"Yeesh! Did I hurt your shoulder?"

"It's not that . . ."

"Oh, I squeezed too hard?" I cringe, though I try not to smile.

His chest shakes as he silently laughs. "You're strong, but not that much. Sam hit me with a tree."

"Ouch, seriously!" I gasp, sitting up, but he pulls me back in. This time, I wrap my arms gently around him, avoiding his left side altogether. "How'd that happen?"

"Never get between brothers arguing over how to build a wooden structure with no instruction manual."

"Yikes." I breathe out, unsure if I should laugh or be worried.

Nestled closer to Marcas, I inhale his earthy sandalwood scent into my nose. How does he smell this good after a long day out in the elements? Did he even have time to shower before coming?

Moments between us like this are few and far between as of late. Some days, I don't even see him. Those nights are restless ones.

"We should get the arch finished by tomorrow night. That's if Sam and Finn stop bickering long enough to make it happen."

Looking up at Marcas, I ask, "You know what Sam needs?"

"A chill pill?" Marcas grins, making me laugh.

"No, a woman—someone to spend all that excess energy on."

"You may be on to something." Marcas' dimples show vibrantly in the light of the screen across the room as he shifts to look into my eyes. His dance wildly, intrigue shifting in their green depths. "But who?"

"Not anyone around here!" I say firmly, recalling Maggie's bothersome entourage, who've already thrown themselves at Sam and been brutally rebuffed. Then there's the ick factor of having anyone I know privy to the secret life I now live.

"You know," Marcas says, drawing me close to him, our faces inches apart. Not wasting the chance, I gently kiss his inviting lips. Then, I put my chin on his shoulder and peer enticingly into his eyes. Surprised, he pauses, his smile widening while his eyebrow rises to a point.

"I'm listening." I grin.

He chuckles and briefly looks over at Jamie, then back at me.

"Sam told me once that I was lucky to have my bride picked for me by the amulet—guaranteeing the perfect fit. He feared someday he'd mess up and make the wrong choice."

"But it's not a guarantee, Marcas. The amulet suggested I'd be a good fit for you and helped you find me, but there was still a chance things wouldn't have worked out between us. What if I couldn't forgive you for how you treated me and refused you? Or, I was what your mother wanted for you but not what you wanted? Would you still be marrying me?"

"I would never take away your chance at the love you deserve. Not for a crown, nor the promise of eternity."

Leaning in, I kiss him tenderly on the lips. This time, he holds me there, needing to kiss me a few more times before letting go.

He then smiles. "And I am extremely grateful you did decide to forgive me."

My cheeks burn pink.

"Anyway, so naturally, I told him if he ever doubted, he should compare the woman's character and standards to those of our mother's." Marcas moves a strand of hair behind my ear. "He would never be wrong if he chose a woman as strong-willed, kind-hearted, and wonderful as she."

Goosebumps cover my arms. It's as if Marcas is saying those things about me.

"Normally, a woman would run screaming if she ever knew a man was comparing her to his mother," I say with a smirk. "But in this case, it would be an honor to come even remotely close to the likeness of such a woman. Having met her only once, I could tell she was a powerful woman—loving and brave."

"Thank you for thinking so."

For a moment, we get lost in each other's eyes. Willing to gaze into his all night, I force myself not to blink. But when mine get too dry to resist, I do, and our link is severed.

Marcas blinks and smiles. "Anyway, so then after we started seeing each other, Sam asked if I'd taken my own advice. Amulet or not, was I sure you were worth all the trouble soon to follow?"

A small, bothersome lump forms in my throat. Do I really want to know his reply?

Taking my hand, he interlocks our fingers. The gesture makes my heart patter in my chest. Looking into my eyes, he whispers, "I told him; I'd leave it all if it meant I'd have you."

My breath catches in my throat. His love is like nothing I have ever experienced before. How did I get so lucky? Thinking of all the events that have led to this exact moment in time, I would go through it all again if it meant I could be this happy here in his arms. To be his one and only.

"Ahem. So, a . . . so what did he say to that?"

"He vowed never to truly date unless he was sure they'd be perfect for him."

"Hence the *'always up for a good time'* vibes he gives. It's kind of hard to see him the same way now. He's not as much the womanizer as I thought."

"Oh, no, he is!" Marcas laughs, and I join in.

"Yeah, but he kind of has to be, right? I don't know if you guys realize it, but you're all kinda hot. I mean, like, *really* hot."

Marcas' smile practically consumes his face. Forget his dimples; I can't even see his eyes because his cheeks are so high.

"Seriously, girls—they *freak*. And if Sam expects to keep his promise, he has to be that way. I can't believe I just defended his behavior!"

"There are obvious sides to him, to be sure. But he also takes his duties very seriously. Of course, except when he took you to Duke's, where you met with Conall."

"Ardan convinced him, remember?"

Marcas' lips purse together as he leans forward for another slice of pizza. "It just makes me angry to think of how close I was to losing you."

"Yeah, but you didn't. Everything worked out."

"I just can't shake this feeling, like something big is about to happen."

"Uh, yeah, our wedding."

"Well, yeah, no, something bad."

My body stiffens slightly as I recall what happened earlier.

"Sorry, don't listen to me. I'm just thinking out loud." He throws his crust into the pizza box, then wipes his fingers with a napkin and tosses it in.

"I wasn't going to say anything, but maybe I should."

His eyes furrow.

"Outside the candy store, this guy with his mom walked past, and the amulet vibrated."

"Did you know him?"

"No, just a tourist, I think. What do you suppose it means?"

Marcas sighs. "Hard to say. Did it feel like before, like with Conall?"

"Not a warning, no. Just . . . a flutter."

"Or a prompting of desire, maybe?" Marcas teases, pumping his eyebrows.

"Tsss, no!"

"You sure? What'd this guy look like?"

I push him playfully, and he laughs.

"I suppose he could've been another wolf," he says, righting himself. "Just in case, I'll have Sam and Finn check around town tomorrow before we meet up."

"Well, he seemed nice at least. I don't think it was a warning about him."

"Maybe. . ." Marcas yawns. "we're both just so exhausted that we don't know which way's up."

I shrug, though I'm not sure that's why. The amulet has never prompted me without a cause before. But at the same time, it wasn't like it was an alarming sort of prod either.

"Yeah, my whole body hurts; leaning over magazines and picture books of flower arrangements all day." An idea pops in my head. "Ooh! Ooh, I got it!" Too excited to hold it in, I hurriedly smack a kiss on Marcas' lips. His breath smells of pepperoni. "You just gave me an idea!"

His surprised eyes squint as he smirks. "All right . . . care to share what you got scheming around in that head of yours?"

"Nope. You'll just have to wait."

He kisses me again, his passion arousing me. Then he pulls away slightly and stares at me intently with his dark, evergreen eyes. "Maybe now?"

Though his intoxicating kisses are usually enough to break me down, they don't this time. "Meh, nope." Then I laugh.

With an accentuated scowl on his face, he grabs my shirt and tugs me close like he's about to rough me up. "It's a good thing I love you." Then he wraps his arms around me and kisses me. Liking his boldness, I match his desire and raise it a degree.

Getting up, he reaches for my hand and pulls me to a stand. He then leads, and I follow to the front door, where he locks it, flicks off the porch lights, and then guides me through the darkened kitchen toward the dim light of my room.

CHAPTER 14

A Break In The Action

The hickory smell of bacon fills my nose.

Reaching for Marcas on the other side of the bed, I find a mound of empty sheets and blankets instead. His absence doesn't surprise me, though. Jamie doesn't cook.

With my robe around me, I open the bedroom door. Jamie is sitting at the table. Dark purplish bags rest under her eyes, and her blonde hair is tangled and frizzy about her face. She holds it back and slowly sips a cup of orange juice then cringes at its tartness.

"Something smells yummy," I muse as Marcas flips eggs in the pan on the stove. "Where'd you get all this?"

He leans in and kisses my cheek. "I figured you'd need something hardy to get you through the morning with your mom."

"Looks like Jamie 'll need it more than me," I say, grinning at her.

Like a zombie, she sluggishly looks at us and rolls her bloodshot eyes. "I resent that comment," she grumbles, her voice rough and gritty. "I just need . . . a minute." She yawns.

I laugh.

"Your couch sucks, by the way," she adds as she rests her head on her folded arms on the table.

"Marcas sleeps on it just fine."

"Yeah, well, I'm a delicate flower," she mumbles from her arms. "And, for the record, I wouldn't even have to sleep on it if Marcas hadn't shown up." She lifts her eyes enough for me to see the glimmer of teasing radiating toward us.

"Hmm, well, it's a wonder either of us could sleep with all that snoring you were doing!" I smirk as I walk to the toaster.

"Not me!"

As I put three slices of bread in and press the handle down, I glance at Marcas.

"Mm-hmm," we hum in unison.

Jamie huffs. "I do not!" Then she sulkily sips her juice, cringing again at the tang.

When the toast pops up, I butter the bread, then place one on each plate Marcas grabs from the cupboard. He adds eggs and bacon to them before I place one in front of Jamie and the other where Marcas will sit. Then I repeat with the last plate, and then I sit. Joining us, Marcas hands us each a fork.

"We gonna see you at Duke's tonight?" Jamie asks Marcas with a mouth full of food.

He shrugs. "Depends on if the boys can get done what's needed. But if Korin doesn't hunt down the things for the ceremony, then there's not much else we can do."

Anxiousness flutters inside me as I glance at my phone. Still no reply from Mom.

"You work them too hard." Jamie grunts.

"What would you have—"

"Jamie, you know we only have a couple weeks left," I say, giving her a hard stare.

She sighs. "So! I miss Finn. Please come tonight. *Please!*"

Marcas pats her hand on the table and grins. "For you, anything."

She swiftly tugs her hand from under his, eyeing him. "That only works on Shae." Then she grins at me before taking another bite of food, her teeth scraping the fork.

My phone suddenly dings twice, a message flashing on the screen.

Of course, sweetie, spend today with Marcas! Things here can wait. But not for too long. Mom adds a winking emoji at the end.

In reply, I text a pink heart emoji.

"Hey, so I was thinking," I say, putting my phone back on the table. "What if we took today off?"

Jamie gawks at me, a bite of egg still resting on the fork in front of her open mouth.

"It's not a bad idea, right?" I ask, looking at Marcas. "I mean, we know Jamie wants it. Don't you? We've been goin-going-goin' for so long. We deserve a break. Spend some time together in the daylight for once."

Marcas slowly swallows his food as he watches me closely. "What about your mom? I thought—"

"She's all for it. Just said so! That is, unless you guys can't afford to take a break."

"Please-*please*, Marcas! Just one day!" Jamie begs.

A warm, inviting smile forms on Marcas' cute, plump, red lips, though he tries to suppress it. The urge to tug him to me so I can lay one on him rages within me. But I somehow resist. He hasn't given his answer yet.

He picks up a piece of bacon off his plate and takes a bite. "Suppose a break every now and then is good for morale. For the sake of productivity, that is." His grin widens in a mischievous, playful way.

"Oh, of course. For productivity." Giddiness bubbles inside me. Finally, a chance to forget it all for just one day.

Jamie squeals with excitement, then hoovers her food down as if she's starving. She takes her plate to the sink, power washes it, spraying water onto the floor, then rushes out of the room.

"Someone's a little excited!" I say as the bedroom door slams shut.

"Little bit." Marcas chuckles as he stands up, walks to the sink, and rinses his dishes. I follow behind him. When he turns around, I am there with a large, excited smile on my face. He wraps his arms around my waist and draws me close. "So." He breathes. "What shall it be? The beach?"

I shake my head.

"Anaconda?"

Again, I shake my head, my smile getting wider the more he tries to guess.

"Missoula? Or I hear there's another ghost town in Garnet. Might be worth checking out."

I frown.

Marcas cringes. "Too soon?" Then he laughs. "All right, give us a hint then."

"Nuh-uh, you'll just have to wait and see. We'll be at your house by ten-thirty. Then we'll go."

"So, it be like that, huh? Holding me captive." Though he squeezes me firmly, I can feel his thrill for the unknown, as if it intensifies his desire for me. Leaning down, he kisses me gently. Soft and sweet, he kisses me again, making my head spin. I wonder if he knows just how much his kisses stir up emotions I never knew I could feel.

"All right, I guess I better warn the boys. They can take longer to get ready than Jamie."

I laugh as Marcas tugs me from the room to the front door. He turns around. "Ten-thirty?"

I nod enthusiastically. "Trust me. You're gonna love it."

After one more quick kiss, he steps off the porch and is already halfway down the walkway before I even feel he's left my arms.

Behind me, I hear Jamie scurry from the kitchen to the bathroom, and then the sound of the shower turning on. Walking back to the kitchen, I grab the rest of the dishes off the table and put them in the sink. My phone at the edge of the table chimes a double ding-ding.

Yo Shae what up?

Hey Niall. Just had breakfast. U?

Same. Made me some waffles! **He puts a tongue sticking out enjoying food emoji**

They were from the freezer weren't they?

Uh so I still had to toast them.

I laugh aloud and shake my head as I move to the couch.

What's the plan for today? I snicker, knowing when he finds out things have changed, he'll freak.

Ugh, the uszh. Would love a break though.

See you at Duke's tonight?

I'll be there. Whether Marcas says I can or not. JK But really I'm going.

Hope so!

Wait! Hold up! Marcas just texted. We're taking the day off! R U SERIOUS!?!?

You're welcome. I text back, smiling, though it's obvious he can't see me.

What're we talkin? Party? Girls? Pls say there'll be girls?

It's a surprise. Tell Finn to pack food for us.

He texts back a mind-blown emoji and the thumbs-up emoji.

Steam follows Jamie out of the bathroom as she walks through to the living room. A large towel is wrapped around her head, like a turban, and one around her body. "Shower's all yours. I'm gonna use your bedroom," she says, grabbing her bag at my feet.

*　　*　　*

Nerves shift in my insides. Never have I ever taken someone other than Jamie to the Glade. Why would I? If seclusion is my desire, anyone else knowing about it would only open myself up for unexpected and most definitely unwanted guests. Not to mention it soon becoming thee hangout spot—número uno for all youth in the area.

Glancing at my phone, I exhale my angst.

"We still have a few minutes, don't we?" Jamie says, dropping two large bags of blankets and throw pillows by the front door. "You said ten-thirty, right?"

"Yeah, but that's when we're supposed to meet at their house. We still have to drive there."

"What? Dang it; sorry, I'll hurry." Jamie then runs around the house, grabbing things and stuffing them into a large recycled tote bag while I take what we've gathered so far out to the car.

She comes rushing down the stairs with one more bag. "This is the last of it, I swear. Lemme just grab my purse, then we'll go."

"Jamie, it's fine, really. Today's supposed to relax us, not stress us out."

She smiles at me. "One sec, okay?" Then she runs back into the house. While I wait, I sift through the playlists on my phone. Just as I press play on a song and put my phone into the cupholder, she hops back in, and I drive on.

For most of the ride Jamie babbles on about how Finn did this for her the other day, and that for her when she didn't expect it, and how much she likes him. Oh, and don't forget how closely he resembles so-and-so from that one movie. Don't get me wrong, I'm thrilled they're so enamored with each other. Her going this long with one guy is huge. But by the time we reach the gravel road leading to Marcas' cabin, I've learned more than I've ever wanted to know about Finn.

I pull up to the parking blocks and turn off the car. While Jamie gets out and rushes up the stairs, I take a moment. Being back here after all that's happened makes me feel weird. I recall the time the boys had Niall traipsing across the yard with one of his brothers on his back after he transitioned, and a sadness shifts inside me. It seems so long ago. A more innocent time compared to what we've been through since. And I believe that was the very last time we had all been together.

"Hey!" Niall pounds on the driver's side window. He laughs at me when I flinch and scream. "You comin' inside?"

"One sec," I pant, my heart racing. He leaves, and I take a deep, calming, centering breath before opening the door and getting out.

As I enter the house, Marcas steps out of his room. "Mo Chroi, you made it! Not too rough of a trip, was it? The road past the gate got washed out during the rain last night."

"It rained?"

"I do believe we were too busy to notice." He winks, then goes down the hall toward the kitchen where I follow close behind him.

The carpet, heated by the sun through the large living room window, warms my feet as I walk across it. Marcas hands me a couple blankets to add to the duffle bag by the couch. "Just in case." He says with a grin.

"See, I told you I had a good idea. Clear skies and abnormally warm temperatures. It's perfect."

"Get off my back. I said I'd take care of it." Niall grumbles, coming from his room into the kitchen.

"You sure we can't ditch the others and find our own private spot?" Marcas mumbles at me, while stuffing a few more things in the bag.

"Dude, you said that days ago. Clean up your junk, or I'm tossing it!" Sam says to Niall, pointing to the pile of clothes on the floor just inside the bathroom.

Giving Marcas a long side glance, I say out of the corner of my mouth, "Maybe we should."

"Marcas, tell Sam to leave me alone!" Niall huffs while sifting through the cupboards grabbing snacks he then shoves into a bag on the counter.

"Guys, we only have one bathroom. You can't keep leaving your stuff all over."

"Then maybe I should move out; save everyone the mess."

Marcas looks at me, the concern on his face matching mine. Then he eyes Niall. "Just clean it up."

"Something's different." I whisper to Marcas. "He's not himself."

Taking a sweatshirt from me, Marcas nudges us toward the big window.

"Where is this talk coming from? He can't move out." I say in a panic.

"It's the transition. Emotions run high right after. Unfortunately, it's not uncommon for our kind to take a break from family for a while because of it."

"No, Marcas, tell him you don't want him to! Make him stay."

"I can't do that. If he needs to, then he should."

"It's not fair. Why does everything keep changing? Why can't it just stay as we like it?"

Marcas laughs a little. "Change is inevitable. But I'm sure he wouldn't be for too long. You'll see."

But Niall can't leave! He means too much to me to not have around.

While Marcas goes back to packing, I go into the kitchen and stand next to Niall.

"What? You gonna give me grief too?" he growls, stuffing crackers and cheese into small sandwich bags, then he presses them closed.

"Niall, no. I wouldn't—"

"Look, I don't need people telling me what to do, all right? I heard Marcas. And I'll clean it up later," he says, forcefully shoving snacks into his backpack.

A prick of annoyance and a smidge of anger tug at me. "Look, Niall, I'm not trying to—I just want to make sure you're all right."

"I'm fine!" He barks loudly.

"Niall," Marcas says firmly from the living room.

Niall's face sinks. "I'm-I'm sorry, I didn't mean—"

"It's okay, Niall," I whisper, pulling him into a hug.

"I don't—I can't."

"Shh, I understand. I mean, Jamie made me listen to her talk about Finn the whole way here. I get it. But we're not all *that* annoying." I feel Niall's body move as he chuckles. "Let's take a break, huh? Get out of here and have some fun, okay?"

He nods as he pulls away. "I'm sor—"

"Hey, Niall, give me a hand with this!" Sam calls from down the hall, making Niall's face harden again.

He breathes out forcefully and scowls. "Coming." Then he leaves.

"Welp, I tried," I say walking to Marcas.

"Don't take it personally. He knows you care."

"Yeah, well."

"Hey, so, the cooler's outside. All packed. You got your keys?" Finn asks, holding out his hand. I give them to him, and he leaves with Jamie following behind with arms full of bags. She smiles as she walks by.

"So, where are we headed, Mo Chroi?"

Pulling my phone from my back pocket, I then paste the coordinates into a message and hit send. "It's a shame Korin and Luc couldn't come. They would have liked where we're headed." I wink.

A second later, Marcas' phone chimes. As he reads it, his eyes light up.

"I thought you guys might like to do a bit of running."

"Are you kidding me?" He says, grabbing me and whirling me around. "But only if you come with," he says, putting me down.

Though I try to hide how excited I am at the idea of running wild with him in the woods, a smirk still shines through.

"Yes! Come on." He grabs me.

"No, Marcas, not now." I laugh pulling back. "When we get there."

Like a playful puppy, Marcas nuzzles my neck and sniffs, making me squirm and laugh. "You're gonna love it."

"I bet I will." I smile alluringly at him. "Help with the stuff first?"

"You heard her! Grab those bags!" he barks, smiling at Tate, Niall, and Sam when they come down the hall.

Like an excited kid about to go out and play, he hurriedly kisses my lips, then smiles so sweetly at me that I almost don't let him leave. Then he turns and rushes out the door. Two seconds later I hear them all howling, like crazy, wild animals as they rush down the gravel road.

"Wild animals," Jamie affirms, shaking her head, then she grabs her purse and goes out the door. I follow close behind.

CHAPTER 15

For The Thrill Of It

Darting alongside my leg, Marcas, in wolf form, jumps to the right, narrowly missing my feet as they stomp hard on the ground. Pine-scented air swishes by my face as I pick up the pace to keep up with him as he veers off to the right.

Tree branches, like blurry green masses, brush against my shoulders as I speed past them. Weaving left, then right, I catch glimpses of Marcas' black fur as he leaps and bounds over all the natural obstacles the forest provides. Like a spirited, playful puppy, Tax flanks him, his tongue hanging out the side of his mouth. When he licks his nose and looks at me, I swear I see him smile.

While I stick to the somewhat packed-down natural animal path, Sam, Tate, and Niall peekaboo between the trees, running to the left of me. Jamie, jumping over a log like a hurdler, follows Finn, who leaps into the air from a fallen tree trunk and lands on the needled forest ground, his paws emitting almost no sound. Jamie flashes a grin at me as she rushes after him.

Feeling a piercing side ache, I slow down, then stop. The tranquility of the forest around me lures me in, mesmerizing me with its beauty as the last of the howls from the others die off without me.

How have I managed to not come up here since finding the amulet? It almost seems inexcusable to have neglected its call for so long. Its comfort has always been a staple in my life, so much so that I can't recall when I didn't find time for it. Even in Seattle, I'd sneak to the Grand Forest on Bainbridge Island to be alone with it. We are soulmates in our nature—these trees and me. Or, my soon-to-be nature, that is. In a few short weeks, I will be a full-fledged wolf, running through this forest with Marcas by my side, the wind ruffling through my fur, bathing me in the rich scent of earth, vegetation, and pine. I want it so bad I can barely stand it.

"Can you believe this?" Jamie pants, coming to my side out of nowhere. Slowing her speed, she soon walks in stride with me.

"Marcas is right; there's nothing like it."

"That'll be you soon. Huh, all free and stuff." There is a hint of sadness in her voice, though she smiles.

"I know—well, you too, right?"

As her smile falters, she shrugs. "Not so sure about that."

"Whaddya mean? Aren't you ecstatic to be a wolf princess?"

She turns as if searching for Finn in the distance ahead of us.

"You haven't asked him?"

Jamie then kneels to tie her shoe even though it doesn't appear untied. "Why bother? He's a mythical creature, a bazillion years older than me, and I'm just the stupid human girl infatuated with him. You'll get married, and then you'll all leave."

My heart aches. "That's not true."

"It's not?" She stands and stares at me. "You *are* leaving, right? Marcas and his brothers, too? What happens to me then, huh? It's not like I can go running after you."

"I just—"

"It's fine, whatever. I'm used to being left behind." She dusts off her pants and starts walking.

"Wait, Jamie. Did Finn say something to make you think you're not going?"

She stops but doesn't turn around. "No. Not exactly. But isn't it obvious?"

"Not how I see it. You're going. I know you are." Walking to her, I put my hand on her shoulder and gingerly turn her around.

She sniffs as tears ripple in her eyes. "He won't . . . want me if I'm not like him."

"Not true." Grabbing her, I pull her into a hug. Her body quakes as she sobs. I want to tell her everything will work out, but I don't know if it will. I hope it does—with everything in me, I do. I just assumed she would be coming with us, so I never thought about what if things didn't work that way? I cannot leave her behind!

217

"Hey, you guys all right?" Finn asks, running up to us in human form again. "Jamie!" He rushes to her, but she does not let go of me.

"Jamie, just ask him," I whisper in her ear. "Anything's better than not knowing."

She shakes her head and buries her face into me.

Looking at Finn, I scrunch my forehead and purse my lips.

His brow deepens. "Jamie, are you all right?" he asks, tugging her shoulder.

She doesn't move.

"Did she get hurt? I thought she was still behind me, so I kept running. Jamie, don't be mad. I didn't mean to leave you behind!"

"It's not that," she says, sounding nasally as she lifts her head. But her eyes do not fall on him.

"Then what? I'll fix it, whatever it is. Just tell me." Though she tries to resist, Finn takes her from me, wrapping his arms around her. "Please, Jamie, talk to me." Her arms do not find their way around him.

Though it's not my place to ask, I swallow my hesitation and do it anyway. "What happens to Jamie when we're gone, Finn?"

"What, like after the wedding? Uh, I figured we'd head back to base. See a few sights along the way."

"To me, Finn. What happens to me?" Jamie sobs, shoving him away, but he grabs her, pulling himself back in.

"What on earth are you on about?" He lifts her chin to make her see him, but her eyes are clenched shut, tears streaming down her face. "Look at me Jamie, please."

She shakes her head.

"What? You don't want me to take you up north, show you off to a few of my buddies. Make 'em all jealous." He winks at me. "I thought that would make you happy, no?"

Bawling harder, she shakes her head again.

Finn looks at me. "What? What am I missing here?" Then he crouches and tries to look into her eyes. "You don't want to go, Jamie? Fine, we'll do something—"

"I'm not a wolf, Finn!" Jamie yells. "This-this isn't going to work!" She pushes him back.

"Hold on. What won't work?" He moves toward her, but she backs away. A look of shock flashes across his face. "Us? We don't work? Are you . . . are you breaking up with me? Hh-how—" His face pales, appearing as though he's about to be sick as he stumbles back, using a tree to steady himself.

"I don't want to, Finn! But I'm just a stupid human and you're . . . you're—"

"Are you insane, Woman?" He exhales forcibly as if he'd been holding his breath for an eternity. "Give me a damn heart attack, thinking you're breaking up with me!" His tone resonates with frustration and utter relief simultaneously. "So, you're not a wolf yet. Big deal. But I'm not ready for our wedding yet, are you? For crying out loud, I can barely handle theirs." He motions to me with a flick of his hand. "But I will, if that's what you want!"

"No." She sobs and wipes tears away. A subtle smile forms on her face, hidden from his view by her hands.

Jamie had heard what I had. *'Our wedding'*, as in, Finn and Jamie forever.

"What do you need me to do, Jamie, huh? Y-You want me to profess my love to you? Shout it through the forest that I'm not going anywhere. 'Cause I will. Let the whole wide world know that I love you and want to marry you. I mean—you honestly thought I could play you like that?"

She shrugs. "I . . . I don't know."

"Oh really? I gave you that impression, did I?" he says, a hint of anger in his tone.

"No, never! I just didn't . . . know."

For a moment, they say nothing. The wind in the trees is the only sound cutting through the silence.

"Jamie, I love you. With all my heart, I do. And if you don't know that by now, then—"

Jamie rushes to him and jumps into his arms. He grabs her face and kisses her long and hard.

"Jamie," he finally says, wiping hair and tears away from her face. "You silly, silly girl, you. Thinking I could live without you. Could leave here and not take you with me. Utter silliness." A smirk forms on his face. "I would—I'd marry you today if I could, but I know we're not ready. Are we?"

A smile shines through her tears as she shakes her head. "But I will be."

"Good." He smiles, his eyes sparkling. "And when that day comes, you will be the most dazzling wolf princess ever." Then he winks and pulls her close, grinning at me over her shoulder.

I smile back, so very happy for them both. Jamie has found her match in every way possible.

"I'm . . . I'm just gonna go." I motion toward the Glade, but Jamie and Finn are too busy making out to notice. Their lip-smacking can still be heard halfway down the trail.

Niall is the first to come into view, followed by Sam and Tate tossing the football. Then I see Marcas lying on a large, multi-colored checkered blanket at the center of the clearing. Tax is resting at his feet. I'm starting to get the impression that he loves Marcas more than me.

"You get lost?" Sam asks, catching the ball as I break the tree line. "Where's Finn and Jamie?" Seeing the smirk on my face, he then rolls his eyes and tosses the ball back to Tate. "Guh, don't blame you for branching out."

"They had a few things to discuss. I was only in the way."

"Discuss—do—same difference." He shrugs, then winks as he catches the ball again.

"Heads!" Niall shouts as a frisbee nearly takes my head off. I retrieve it and spin it back to him. Missing Niall, it flings off to the left. While he goes to get it,

Marcas uses his seductive smile to lure me over. When Niall turns around to toss the frisbee to me again, he stops short, finding me almost to him.

"I-I thought we were playing." He frowns.

"Raincheck? I'm kinda spent."

"Hey, yeah, no, no worries." He tosses the frisbee on the ground at his feet. "I think I'll go for another run anyway." Then he takes off without waiting for a reply. Tax scrambles to his feet and takes off after him, then stops to watch Sam and Tate with the ball.

Niall's abrupt change of plans sends a tweak of guilt upon me. Time with him has been null these last few weeks. I'm sure he feels the disconnect as much as I do, but with everything that needs to be done, it's hard to avoid it. I should probably carve out some much-needed Niall time today before it's too late.

The rumbling of hunger gurgles like an erupting volcano in my stomach.

"Hungry?" Marcas smirks while adjusting the pillows propping his head up. "There's food in there." He nods towards a white cooler.

Lifting the lid, I rummage through the ice water and drinks floating in it to find a ham and cheese sandwich double wrapped in plastic bags with my name on it. Slamming the lid closed, I then walk over to Marcas. "Hey, I think you're lying over where I found the amulet."

"Here? No kidding." He gestures for me to join him on the blanket. I take two nibbles of my sandwich and sit. Although now that I've had a taste, I am ravenous for it. Practicing restraint, I take a larger bite rather than tearing into it like the crazed, starving beast.

"How'd you find this place anyway? It's gorgeous here."

"It's my uncle's land. He lets me come whenever I feel like it. I guess that'd be all the time." I chuckle to hide my embarrassment at how pathetic I sound for having an almost nonexistent social life until lately.

"Interesting."

"I love how peaceful it is here." I sigh, looking around. The golden grass is knee-high; well, at least those areas that Sam and Tate haven't managed to stomp flat. And the jagged mountains seem to be richer with greens for this time of year. The Aspen leaves have yet to start turning orange. Although, I suppose it's been a while since I've been here this time of year. The summer after graduation may have been the last. Perhaps I do not recall them accurately.

Stuffing the last bite of my sandwich into my mouth, I snuggle in, resting my head between Marcas' shoulder and upper chest. I crave this position. We go together like two halves of a heart.

"Your uncle . . . would that be your—?"

"Mom's brother, yeah. Before him, my grandfather owned it."

"Taxidermist?"

I laugh. "Yep."

"*Very* interesting."

"What is?" I say, squeezing him closer.

"I'm not positive, but I think I've dreamt of this place before," Marcas says casually, though I sense there is a hidden meaning behind his thoughts.

"Really! And you've never been here before?"

"I think I'd remember seeing a beautiful woman hangin' around, if I had." He grins a sheepish smile that makes my arm hairs tingle.

"Do you remember the dreams?" I ask, wondering how deep our link to this place goes. Having found the necklace in a place he's also dreamt about almost seems too purposeful to be coincidental.

"It's not so much about the dream itself, but rather how I feel when I'm here."

"Like there's a powerful hum that vibrates right through you?" I ask, knowing the feeling all too well.

"The ground feels electrified."

"Grandpa used to say it's because of the gems in the mines on the property. Like they're supernaturally charged or something. But I don't know. It feels deeper than that. It's just—I feel connected to this place, like . . ."

"It's a part of you."

"Yes! That's weird to say, though, right?"

"Not at all." He smiles.

"Could it be supernatural then if you're a wolf shifter and feel it too?"

"Fáelad," Marcas corrects me.

"Right, Fáelad," I repeat in the hopes of committing it to memory.

"I suppose. If you found the amulet here, it could mean it's Fae holy ground."

"My Mom?"

Marcas smiles and squeezes me close, then kisses my forehead. "Fae, as in fairy kind." He can't help but chuckle, though he tries to hold it in.

"Huh, I thought you were kidding about that. There's actually a fairy queen?"

He nods. "I hope to introduce you to her someday. She's amazing."

"Fairies. . ." I say, astounded. "Do you see any now?"

Marcas laughs. "Not unless there's a fairy portal around here I don't know about."

"Portal?" I sit up. "Seriously? Are you teasing me?"

As he sits up, he forces his smile away. "Never, Mo Chroi. The portals lead to the fairy realm, though none exist in America."

My eyes narrow in on him to spot if he's lying, but when his eyes smile genuinely back, like when he told Jamie and me their secret, I know he's not. "All right. Then name one place."

"I would, but it's forbidden."

"Uh, even to your future queen?"

"Like I said, I'll take you there someday." The gentle yet finiteness in his tone warns me not to pry any further, so I don't.

"Fine." I kiss him on the lips, then smile. "I'll wait."

He lays me back on the blanket and uses his arms out to the sides of my head to prop himself up so his face is over mine. A sweet, alluring smile widens his lips. "I just had an idea."

"Marcas, not here!"

He laughs and uses his body and arms to prevent me from moving. "Not that. About the wedding. Though, what you thought of does sound enticing." Gradually lowering his head, he kisses me. "Maybe later." Then he grins.

Breathless from his incredibly persuasive kiss, I ask, "S-so what's the idea then?"

"We should have the wedding here."

"Here. . ? But what about the other place? All that work? Won't Sam—"

"Won't Sam what?" Sam asks, walking up to us along with Tate and Tax.

My skin flushes warm, having been caught in an intimate position with Marcas. Trying to ignore my burning cheeks, I clear my throat. "Marcas wants to have the wedding here."

"*We* want it here." Marcas corrects me.

Sam's happy features flatten, though he does not speak.

Marcas sits up, letting me do the same.

"It was just an idea, Sam. We don't . . . we don't have to change—"

"No," Sam says, narrowing his eyes at me.

"Sam, if Shae wants it here—"

"Marcas, it's all right. The other place is perfect. Sam, it's fine—"

"I said no!" Sam says, turning his back on us.

A cold sensation chills me like someone has sucked all the warmth out of the air. Marcas looks at me, his lips pressed firmly together.

"It's, it's fine, Marcas," I say, shaking away the need to get emotional.

Sam turns around, the deep scowl on his face almost too hurtful to look upon. But then it shifts into a grin. "I was thinking we could move the arch there." He points to the area he and Tate had packed down. "And line the chairs coming out this way. Hang lights all around and put the battery generator there. And, of course, the buffet—"

Jumping up, I almost punch him, but I tackle-hug him instead. "Thank you, Sam!" The tightness in my throat threatens to take my voice away, but I swallow it back down. "Thank you."

"I could never say no to you," he says in my ear. "After all you've been through—done for us—for Marcas. Besides, your wedding should be where you want it." He then grins mischievously at me. "Gotcha, though, didn't I?"

"Cruel, Sam, truly cruel!" I say, slugging his arm. Then I laugh and hug him again, because it's better than beating him up, which I so badly want to do now.

"It looks like we've got our work cut out for us," Sam says, stepping back with his eyebrows raised at Marcas.

"I tell you what. You get it all here, and I'll build it!" Marcas says, extending his hand to Sam.

"Deal!" They clasp each other's forearms and move in for a bro hug, patting each other on the back twice before letting go.

"Hey! What'd we miss?" Niall says, walking up, followed by Finn and Jamie.

"Guess who gets to move all those chairs and set them up here?" Sam says, then laughs when Niall's face falls.

"Wha—all by myself?"

Everyone but me and Niall laughs. I feel bad that changing the venue creates more work for them, but at the same time, having my wedding in the one place I am the most at peace makes it worth the effort.

"We got you." Tate slaps Niall on the shoulder. "Or at least Finn and Sam do since I'm taking off tomorrow."

"Wait, you are? Since when?" I ask, feeling the sting of being left out.

"Korin called earlier. He needs me. Don't worry, we'll be back for the big night."

"You better!"

"I'm looking forward to it." He smiles.

"All right, it's settled! Now, who wants ice cream?" Sam yells, then darts for the red cooler several feet away. Niall, Tax and the others run after him while Marcas brings me close and wraps his arms around me from behind. As we gaze across the grassy space in front of us, I hold his arms.

"It'll be perfect. Just imagine tiny white twinkling lights crossing from tree to tree." His breath moves my hair next to my ear as he talks.

"Large wooden lanterns on the tables with candles and flowers inside." As I try to picture where they will all go, I hear Sam and Finn in the background fighting over the only fudge bar dipped in peanuts that Sam has clutched in his hand. And Jamie yelling at them to stop being so childish and share. "And a buffet table with food fit for kings back there," I add, pointing to a space behind us.

"Don't forget the dignitaries from around the globe gathered here to celebrate our union."

"They will?" I suddenly feel less than worthy of having such an event.

"Well, those who aren't otherwise engaged."

"Will they bring gifts?" I smile, imagining what sort of things they'll lavish us with.

"Definitely."

"Like what?"

"I'll let you wait and be surprised."

"It all sounds so perfect." I sigh.

"Almost as perfect as getting married in the fairy realm."

I turn in his arms so I can see the look of teasing on his face. "Fairy realm or not, it will be magical."

He chuckles, then kisses me. When I open my eyes, he is looking at me, his intensely green eyes gleaming. "So much more than you know."

CHAPTER 16

Nightfall

Jamie pops her head out of the bathroom with a brush in her hand. "Time check?"

"Six-fifty. You've still got time."

"Ooh, aren't you gorgeous?" She beams at me, then darts back into the bathroom. "Grab the hoop earrings off the table by the couch and wear those," she yells. Finding them, I put them on and stand by the bathroom door, watching her briskly apply blush to her cheeks. "Is it too pink? It's new, and I'm not sure it's me."

"Try rubbing it in more and adding a lighter hue higher up. Like there." I point to the top of her cheekbone.

She blends the color into her skin with her fingertips, then brushes a light, sparkly shimmer on top, making her already slender cheekbones pop. "Brilliant! Since when do you know so much about makeup?"

"Since forever. I just don't always wear as much."

"All right. Okay. Fair enough."

In my hand, my phone dings twice.

"If that's Marcas, tell him I'm gonna need, like, fifteen more minutes."

When I see a message from Niall instead, I push my disappointment away.

Yo sleepyhead u up yet?

Yes, Derry, I am. Thanks for asking. I include an emoji face with its tongue sticking after it, then add, *And FYI it was a 30 min nap, not one of your 2 hour ones!*

Grrr, that middle name. I never should have told you. Why can't I have something cool like Derek or Nash? And it was an hour nap this time. Thank you very much!

Cos ur not awesome like that Niall. LOL!

. . . flashes in a dotted sequence on the screen as if he is returning a long reply.

They disappear.

Niall, I'm kidding.

The dots return, then disappear again.

Niall?

The space stays empty.

Worry stirs in the pit of my stomach. Not again. Just how long is this new transformation attitude going to last? His lightheartedness has taken a major blow. Giving a scowl here and a complaint there when he would have otherwise laughed it off. Sometimes I wonder if this new Niall comes with mood swings *and* an ego he can't quite navigate yet.

Sighing, I put my phone away.

"Everything okay?" Jamie asks, fixing her tight red belly shirt.

"It's Niall."

She rolls her eyes and continues to get ready.

A second later, I hear more dings, but I'm afraid to check. Almost.

'I've never told you this but . . . There's a pause before another message comes through. *I love you, like LOVE you love you. (Don't tell Marcas)*

Flaming heat rushes across my face.

"What's he saying now?" Jamie groans, leaning over to see my phone, but I cover it discreetly.

"Nothing, just, you know, Niall being Niall." Then I move to the living room and scour the message repeatedly looking for a hint of a joke.

No, Niall, please! My heart spastically pounds away in my chest. Nothing! Not a single clue of a tease. My stomach flops as my hands begin to sweat. This-this can't be happening. How do I even respond?

I

Delete.

You can't be

Delete, delete, delete.

We could never . . .

With the weight of our friendship hanging in the balance, no words seem to fit. Fear of how he will react grips me. What should I do?

What? Nothing to say? **Niall texts.** *Come on you must have known? Noticed the way I am when you're near me. I thought now that I've changed, I'd have a better chance with you.*

Erasing my unsent text, I then type, *Niall, you're like a brother to me.* But it feels stiff, so I delete it. *Don't do this! You know I love Marcas!* Even that sounds lame, so I erase it too, and bite my lip.

??? **Niall texts again.**

Grrr, Niall! You want an answer I can't give. Please be joking. Please!

Niall, we really should tal—

STOP!' **Pops up on the screen.** *DON'T ANSWER THAT! SAM!!!!! He stole my phone while I was in the bathroom!*

A cold rush of relief washes over me, followed by the sudden urge to hunt Sam down and kill him.

Deleting my message, I then pound out my reply. *That punk! Get him! GET HIM!*

Already did. Bet he had u good there for a second though, didn't he? LOL! Sweating bullets. Like u need another man after your heart.

Yeah, right. I knew it wasn't you. That's why I didn't respond. Why give you . . . **delete** *. . . him the reaction he was wanting?*

LOL, sure u did.

Don't you have work to do?

Ouch, testy! And no, I'm off tonight, remember? Op, Marcas says to tell you we're coming! See you soon!

I quickly send back a thumbs up.

Jamie leans over me and peeks out the window. "Are they coming or what?"

Still feeling the trauma of Sam's tactless prank, I exhale, "Leaving now," and drop my phone on my lap.

Jamie plops on the couch next to me. Her curly locks bounce fluidly about her face. "Marcas all better then?"

"Seemed to be. He ran a lot today. I think he's missed it."

"It was amazing, watching them move like that. I can't believe we did that with them!"

"I can't wait until that's us."

"What do you think it'll be like being queen?"

"Not sure. We've been so caught up with the wedding that I haven't thought to ask."

"Royalty duties most likely. Kissing babies and planting trees."

"I guess. If they even do that kind of thing."

She shrugs. "Well, if they do, then have fun with that." She grins and pats my leg.

"Uh, you'll be there with me, my lady in waiting."

"Hah, only until I get married."

"Sorry, your devotion is for life. Sam says so. And that will be for a very . . . *very* long time." I cackle.

"Keep dreaming." Jamie laughs too.

"Speaking of weddings. . ."

She gleams at me as if unable to hide the pure joy radiating through her body. "He loves me!" She squeals.

"Yeah, I figured. He said, 'Wedding,' Jamie. *Wedding!*"

She sighs dreamily. "I know." Then she squeals again, and I join in. "It's not official though, but I'm fine with that. Just knowing that's where it's headed is enough for me!"

"Well, I'm happy for you both."

"Oh, but, Shae, I promise I won't steal your thunder. You won't hear a peep out of me about this, I swear."

"I'm not worried." Though I know the moment it's official, she'll be on it like white on rice. Here's to hoping it's not too soon after mine, though. I'd like a bit of a honeymoon first. After the time Marcas and

I've had, we deserve the time away. "You're dreaming about it right now, aren't you?"

She shakes her head, but the smile she is suppressing breaks through till her shake becomes a nod. "Who are we kidding? I've been planning it since I met him!" We both laugh.

"Then it's a good thing you'll be with me tomorrow. Dive right into it!"

"No, Shae, I'm serious; I will not make this about me!"

"Mhmm, if you say so."

A second later, I hear the bustle of feet trekking on the gravel driveway outside. Excitement buzzes through me. Then a knock at the door as it opens.

"You ladies, decent?" Sam chimes and lets the door creak open, an eager smile on his face. Laying eyes on us, fully dressed and sitting on the couch, he frowns and shoves the door the rest of the way open. "All ready, I see. Just my luck," he adds under his breath.

Crinkling my nose at him, I say, "Nice to see you too, Sam," as I stand. When will he learn? Girls don't like degrading womanizing jokes about men finding us in scandalous, naked conditions.

"What'd ya expect, us just standing here naked, waiting for you?" Jamie scoffs, also standing up.

Sam's face perks up. "It could happen!"

"You git, that's my girlfriend," Finn says, having come through the front door. Punching Sam in the arm, he adds, "And our future sister. Yuck! No offense, Shae." He grabs Jamie and pulls her into a side hug. "Not you either, babe." His eyebrows pulsate up and down, making her giggle and slap his rock-hard pec, where her hand then remains.

Suddenly remembering Sam's horrid joke, I reach over and punch him right where Finn had before.

"Ow! What's that for?"

"You know!" I eye him hard.

His distorted, shocked features shift to a sly grin as he rubs his arm. "Worth it, though," he mumbles, then jumps back and yells, "Hey!" when I try to hit him again.

Behind Sam, Niall steps up and gives him another quick, sharp punch in the exact same spot, then titters and diverts to the side when Sam whips around trying to swing at him.

"Will you people stop punching me?" Sam growls loudly, stumbling backward. Marcas stops him from bumping into him.

"Suppose they would if you stopped deserving it." Marcas' eyes light up while the rest of us laugh.

Scowling at us all, Sam walks back outside.

*   *   *

240

As Jamie and I push Duke's heavy double doors open and step inside, we are greeted with the usual wall of loud music and strobing lights. Although bands don't perform on stage this late in the season, the rhythms and atmosphere are still cool enough to hold their own.

Not many people are around either, now that the summer is almost over. Once into August, not only do the average temperatures drop to frigid degrees at night, but schools across the states will start back up by the end of the month. Some people take a last-minute vacation before that happens, although not as many as during the summer. At the moment, I sort of like that we have our hangout back.

A chill of remembrance dances up my arms as one particular bothersome tourist who couldn't take no for an answer comes to mind. Will my memory of this place be forever tainted by what happened here?

Sam and Niall grab a few pool tables while Marcas, Jamie, and I get drinks.

"Shae!" Trent says from behind the bar. His eyes smile as brightly as his lips. But when he sees Marcas, they lose some of their luster. "Marcas."

"Hey, Trent. How's it going?"

"Uh, yeah, things are, things are good, I guess." Trent's eyes shift between me and Marcas.

Noticing, Jamie grabs Marcas' arm and says, "Come on, let's go pick some tunes!" Then she drags him away before he's able to protest.

Hopping onto a bar stool, I spin around to face the counter. "Um, Trent, is everything okay?"

He huffs and glares at Marcas behind me while wiping a glass with a white bar rag. "How can you be with that guy after how he treated you? It's not right, Shae. You deserve better."

Swallowing down the need to spastically defend Marcas' honor because it will only add to Trent's suspicions, I purse my lips instead. "It's true, he was pretty awful that night. But that's not who he really is; I promise."

His brow scrunches into a vee. "So, you, you just forgive him after what he said—how he treated you? Because if you were mine, I'd never—"

"I know," I say, stopping him from confessing what I've dreaded him doing since high school. Any girl would be lucky to have the affections of a guy like Trent, but he isn't for me. Never was. And the last thing I want him doing now is reigniting old feelings—ones I will never reciprocate. "Thank you for looking out for me. I appreciate it, really, I do. But there's more to that night than you know. Things that I can't talk about. You just have to trust me that it's all good now."

"Are you in some kind of trouble, Shae? Seriously, tell me! Does he . . . hurt you—because I swear—?" He slams his hand, still gripping the towel, onto the countertop.

"No, Trent," I say, looking around to see if anyone noticed. "Nothing like that at all. Marcas saved me."

Huffing, he rolls his eyes.

"No, I mean it; he actually saved my life that night from this guy out back."

"Wha—here? Who—what happened?" His nostrils flare, and his jaw clenches. Anger and concern run deep in his blue eyes.

"I'm sorry, I can't . . . I can't tell you anything more."

"But you would, though, right? If you needed help?" He takes my hand and squeezes it gently as his pensive eyes analyze my face.

Beaming warmly at him, I nod. "In a heartbeat. Please, Trent, be happy for me. And give Marcas a chance to show you he's not so bad."

Pressing his lips together, he then smacks his lips. "If you say he is"—he smiles—"then I guess I can give him a shot."

"Thank you, Trent!"

"Yeah, yeah," he says as he lets go of my hand and flips the towel over his shoulder. "So, what'll it be?"

Giving a smile so wide my cheeks hurt, I shrug. "Surprise me."

He chuckles and goes about mixing something.

"Hey, are you off soon?"

"In about twenty minutes. Why?"

"You should hang out with us after."

"Yeah . . . yeah, maybe I will." He wipes the counter off, then puts a caramel-colored drink in front of me.

"Thanks! See ya," I say, hopping off the stool. Grabbing my drink, I then walk to the Jukebox by the stage. Seeing me coming, Jamie takes off for Finn at the pool tables, while Marcas punches in the code for a song and then turns around.

"How's Trent?"

"Not too fond of you at the moment."

Clicking his cheek, Marcas takes my drink. "I was afraid of that." Then he sips it. "Should I be concerned?" he asks, handing it back to me.

Of him liking you? I don't think so. Of his jealousy of you? Perhaps.

"Nah, he'll see soon enough there's nothing to fret about."

Marcas' lips curl up, though his eyes hold a smidge of concern. Then again, it's Marcas—always on his guard. "I'm heading over. Are you coming?"

"After I pick out a few songs first. Something that goes well with a hardy butt-kicking. 'Cause, you know, I'm gonna be doing a bit of that in a minute." I wink, and he cracks up as he walks away.

Turning back to the machine, I start perusing my options. *Sift, sift, sift, Click—Gold on the Ceiling (The Black Keys). Sift,* then *click—Money Maker (also TBK). Sift, sift, sift, click—Eye of The Tiger (Survivor).* I smirk, hoping that one will play just as I get Sam right where I want him. *Sift, sift,* then *click—The Final Countdown (Europe).*

As I continue to find more songs, the sense of being watched makes the hairs on the back of my neck prickle. Looking at the bar, I see Trent busy with things behind the counter. Over at the pool tables, I notice Jamie laughing with Finn while Niall decides on a stick with Marcas. Turning around, I methodically scour the tables and make eye contact with a shadowy figure in the corner. A cold panic washes over me as I pointedly turn back to the Jukebox. My breath catches in my throat when the person gets up and walks my way.

'*Marcas!*' I scream in my head as I breathe rapidly through my nose. Be brave, Shae; you're a wolf, remember? Wolves aren't wimps.

"Is that you?" a man questions, a hint of an Irish accent to his familiar voice as he stops beside me. His sparkling blue eyes dance with recognition when I glance at him. "Aye, the candy shop, right?"

"Oh, yeah, hi," I say as relief washes over me.

Once again, the amulet against my collarbone subtly vibrates, officially debunking the possibility of it being a coincidence. Who is this guy? Why does the amulet call out to me in such a cryptic way whenever he is near? Should I fear him, or is there a connection between us I don't yet know about?

"Sorry about my mum earlier. I'd say it was nap time, but she's pretty much like that all the time." He smirks.

"Yeah, she, uh, she seemed super . . . friendly."

While stroking his red curly hair back with his fingers, he smolders at me. "So, you're from here then? That's cool."

Trying not to get sucked into his flirtatious trap, I scrunch my nose. "I suppose so. And you're just passing through, I take it?"

"Aye, arrived just yesterday," he says, then checks his watch and reads a notification.

Over the guy's shoulder, I spot Marcas. Watching us with a keen stare, he starts walking over.

"Anyway, my parents are trying to connect with an old friend in the area. Do you know—"

"Shae," Marcas says, stepping up to us. "Sorry to interrupt. Just wanted to let you know we're ready to play whenever you are." His smile is warm, yet his eyes hold a speck of rigidity.

"Oh, um, yeah, I'll, uh, I'll be a sec."

Marcas nods and clears his throat, then rotates his shoulders back, popping his neck while giving me a prodding stare.

"Right, sorry, Marcas, this is uh—um."

"Lorcan."

"Right, Lorcan."

"Lorcan," Marcas repeats. His lips extend wide, his eyes giving a piercing stare as he reaches out his hand. His forearm strains, accentuating every muscle group extending up his arm as he vigorously shakes Lorcan's hand. "Pleasure. So how do you two know each other?"

"We, uh, we met briefly outside the candy shop yesterday," I say, raising my eyebrows at Marcas, hinting that this is the guy I told him about before; however, his scrunched brow gives me doubt that he gets it.

"Where are you in from, Lorcan?" Marcas says, narrowing one eye at him while folding his arms across his chest. I try not to notice his bulging biceps, but I think he's flexing.

"We just spent a week in Yellowstone. Breathtaking there, isn't it?"

"Truly. So, how long are you planning on staying in town?"

Arching an eyebrow, Lorcan looks at me, then back at Marcas. "Ah, right." He nods. "No need to worry there, mate. We're in, then out. A day or so, tops."

"Right, good." Marcas' tone deepens. "Well, we should go; we don't want to keep everyone waiting.

Shae." Placing his hand on the small of my back, he motions with his head toward the others and starts guiding me that way.

"I-It was nice meeting you, Lorcan. I hope you enjoy your stay."

"Thanks for the friendly chat." He grins and winks, then walks in the direction of the bar, but then veers right and out the front doors.

Slapping Marcas on the shoulder, I huff. "Was that necessary?"

Raising his eyebrow to a point, he smirks. "What?"

"Right. . . That wasn't you playing alpha?"

Though he attempts to conceal it, his mouth twitches with a side smirk. "Uh, no; I was being polite. Besides, you were frightened before. For all I knew, he was about to hurt you."

"Fair enough; I'll give you that." Getting up on my tiptoes, I kiss him on the lips. "But there's no need for jealousy, Marcas. You already have my heart." Then I wink, my eyes sparkling up at him before I walk away.

"I was not jealous." He walks faster to keep up with me.

"It's no big deal. At least you're cute when you are."

"Are what?" Jamie asks when we reach the tables.

Pursing his smirking lips, Marcas eyes flicker in protest.

Giving a lopsided grin back, I say, "He's terrified of getting his butt kicked. Speaking of; you ready, Sam?"

"What? Nuh-uh, I'm not playing you. You cheat," Sam says, shoving off the chair he's leaning on.

"Scared of a little competition?" As if purposefully timed, *Eye of the Tiger* booms through the speaker overhead, and I laugh.

"Oh, it's so on!" Sam growls and rips the stick out of Niall's hands. "Rack 'em up!"

Niall takes out the balls and triangles them where they go with the black guide.

"Room for one more?" Trent says, coming up beside me.

"Hi! Sorry, this one's between me and Sam."

Observing my broad grin, Sam, standing rigid across the table from us, snarls his lip, his jaw clenched.

"Out for blood, I see." Trent sniggers. "I sure hope you left your wallet at home, dude."

"You're first, Sam." I motion to the table. He huffs, then positions himself at the far end, bent over, stick poised in hand.

Crack!

"You up for a round?" Marcas offers Trent a stick.

"Sure," he says, taking it and smiling. "But I give fair warning. I've had an excellent teacher." Then he winks at me.

Marcas chuckles. "Thanks for the heads up."

A comforting warmth washes over me as I watch them converse while starting their game. Now, why doesn't Trent stir such territorial behavior in Marcas like with that guy? With all the history between us, Trent could easily be a threat, with his thick black hair, blue eyes, and tattoos. Girls go nuts for them. Then again, I should consider myself lucky that Marcas doesn't know about Trent's secret affection for me. Another love triangle is not what this girl needs.

"Are you gonna go or what?" Sam glowers.

"Dude, you should probably play nice. She holds your fate in her hands." Finn says as he and Jamie walk over to Marcas' table.

"Finn calls the next game, Shae."

"Uh, no, he doesn't!" Finn hollers back.

Sam and I laugh.

CHAPTER 17

Trouble Times Three

We arrive at my parent's house a little before eleven thirty.

"I'm so glad you came to help," Mom says, hugging Jamie when we walk through the door.

"Anytime! You know I love this kind of stuff." Jamie grins, then looks at me, where I see the extra flicker of excitement in her lashes as they flutter.

Mom's white furball of a dog barks at our feet nonstop until she shooshes him out of the room. A second later I hear the plastic flap of its dog door in the kitchen swing as it goes outside. It's a good thing

I left Tax at home, otherwise, I do believe he would have chewed the barking bandit like a tennis ball just to stop its incessant yapping.

"How was yesterday? Everything work out?"

"Yes, definitely! It was just what we needed; thanks again, Mom," I say while we take our shoes off at the bench inside the door.

"Well, I hope you came ready to work. We got more RSVPs yesterday. And I finished this." From behind the hutch in the dining room, she pulls out a whiteboard labeled 'Seating Chart' in bright pink, glittery letters at the top. Big circles representing tables have little yellow blank sticky labels next to each of them. "We should nail this sucker down by today! And if anyone else responds, well, they'll just have to sit at the overflow table."

"And throw off the ratio? You rebel!" I laugh.

Teasing me with a playful snarl, she lays the board on the table. "We also need to finalize the centerpieces. I'm heading to Missoula today or tomorrow to pick up supplies."

"Mom, you don't have to do that. Marcas and I can handle it."

With her arm around me, she pulls me close and smiles. "But we're a team, remember? Besides, you'll have plenty to do while I'm gone."

I frown, and she laughs.

"All right, Mrs. Donnelly, put me to work." Jamie rubs her hands together. "Let's knock this stuff out!"

"For crying out loud, Jamie; you're a grown woman. Call me Fae."

Jamie's cheeks redden. "Right, sorry."

Mom guides Jamie to the other side of the table and opens some magazines with different colored tabs. "We need fourteen cohesive centerpieces."

Jamie's eyes widen. "*Fourteen*?"

"Don't look at me. Mom sent the invites. You, Trent, and the boys are my people."

"We've lived in a lot of places over the years and made a lot of friends. It would be rude not to invite them to our only daughter's wedding."

"You forgot to mention also inviting the whole town."

Scrunching her nose at me, she says, "Friends are friends, no matter where they live or how long it's been since you've seen them."

"Let 'em come. Means more presents and cash." Jamie pumps her eyebrows.

"All right, you two; time to work." Mom points to the board and the magazines at the same time, then leaves. Returning a few minutes later, she places another stack of magazines next to Jamie who's too busy jotting things down on sticky notes to look up, but she manages to mumble, "Thank you."

"Who's Marcas' best man again?" Mom asks, now on my side of the table where I've been staring blank-faced at the dang chart since she left.

"Korin, his best friend."

"That's right, from Guatemala or someplace like that."

"Around Panama, I think," Jamie says, not bothering to stop writing.

"Any plus ones I should know about?"

Maggie's name pops into my head, and I smother a smile. She wishes she were a plus one for Korin. "Not that I know of, but I'll ask."

"All right, well, I'll be in the kitchen making us a snack if you need anything."

"No, Mom, stay! I can't do this by myself!"

"Really, Shae." She takes the paper and examines it. "Start with this side of the family." She taps on the left column—my father's family. "Knowing how well they get along, let's put them in pairs around each table. That should keep the noise down—for a little while, at least." She winks. "And anyone under twelve at the kid's tables. Teens at that one." She points to two tables across the room from each other, then hands me back the paper and pats my shoulder. "See, you've got this! And if you want, I'll check it later." Then she walks away.

With a heavy gulp, I smother my apprehension and start placing names.

Hyper-focused on our tasks, Jamie and I work in silence for a while.

When the doorbell rings, Jamie and I jump right out of our focused thoughts.

"I'll get it!" I yell toward the kitchen. "My brain's fried anyway," I mumble, walking to the front door. About a foot away from the door stands a tall, thin man with dark brown eyes. To his right is a stout woman with gray hair wearing a familiar unpleasant grimace. Beside her is, "Lorcan?"

"Shae! I—you . . . live here?" Confusion flashes in his eyes.

"Wh-what are you doing—"

A deep-throated grunt comes from his mother, making Lorcan straighten not only his posture but the smile on his face.

The older man steps forward and takes his tweed cap off, then runs a hand through his dark brown hair. "Howya lass. Name's Jarlath. This be Brigid, my wife, and it seems you know our son, Lorcan. Pardon our interruption, but we've been lookin' for the right gaff. Would Mr. and Mrs. Dale Donnelly be livin' here?" His thick Irish accent holds a pleasant tone; easy to understand like Lorcan's. Not like the swallowing-your-tongue sort of sound I recall his wife having.

"Umm. . ." I glance from him to his wife and am met with a deep sneer as her eyes burrow into mine. It sends chills down my arms. I divert my gaze back to the man. "Uh, yes . . . yes. Is she expecting you?"

"She'd rightly be, I'd imagine," Jarlath says with a smile.

Not entirely convinced, I hesitate before saying, "Please, come in. I'll go get her." Opening the door, I let them pass into the house.

"What are you doing here?" I whisper to Lorcan, having been the last to come through. But before he can reply, his mother gives us both a death glare. "This way." I lead them into the living room, where they sit on the long couch facing the matching loveseat.

Jamie comes in from the adjoined dining room just as my mom enters from the kitchen.

"Shae, who was at the—" Mom gasps, and the towel in her hand falls to the floor.

I rush over and pick it up, then hand it back. "They said you knew they were coming." But her stiff body and wide eyes tell me they had lied.

"Howya Fae. It's been a wee minute, hasn't it?" Jarlath says with bright eyes, though his lips are now pressed.

"Don't you look grand?" Brigid says, her deep, raspy voice carrying with it a smidge of asperity in the form of a high-pitched lift at the end of her compliment.

"I—" Swallowing, then licking her lips, Mom twists the towel and glances at Brigid.

"Don't be gawkin' at me." The woman huffs. "Surely you'd be gettin' our messages."

Messages? The letter I gave Mom?

"Now Brigid, dear. See Fae's wee bab in the light. How she's bloomed. Quite the sweet, fine thing, isn't she?" Jarlath says while putting his hand on his wife's. Instead of a smile, she scrunches her long nose at me as if smelling something foul.

Feeling the weight of her judgment, I try not to sneer back.

Who are these people?

To stop Mom's death-grip twisting of the towel, I grab her hand. "Mom. . ."

"Yes." She clears her throat and looks at me. "All, all grown up. And just about to head out with Jamie, weren't you, sweetie?" Her lips curl into a large fake smile as her eyes shift to the front door.

Worry flops about inside me as I notice a hint of anxiousness in my mother's eyes.

Through a side glance, I try to gauge what Jamie is thinking, but her features are as guarded as mine. "We . . . we could stay if you—"

"But what about your appointment?" Her eyes pierce me with a rigid stare as she presses her lips together and forces a flat smile. "You shouldn't miss it. *Marcas* is waiting."

Warning bells keep ringing in my head.

There's protection in numbers, Mom. Why do you insist we leave?

"C'mere, Fae; sit down with us. Please, we have much to discuss." Jarlath motions to the loveseat across from them.

"Girls, I'm sure you'll be enjoyin' what we're here fer," Brigid says with a hint of smug satisfaction. When we don't move, she grunts. "I insist. *Sit.*"

No longer having a say, we follow my mom to the loveseat, where she and I sit with Jamie taking the armrest.

Lorcan, sitting stiffly next to his mother, stares at his hands on his lap like they are the most captivating thing he's ever seen.

Why didn't he tell me last night about coming here? Did he not know, or was he told not to mention it? Was that what he was about to say when Marcas showed up?

The amulet vibrates again, stirring panic within me. What is it trying to tell me? What am I supposed to know?

"Where be Dale this fine day?" Jarlath asks.

"Out of town, I'm afraid, at a car show in Missoula." Mom presses a smile as she grabs my hand. "We don't expect him back until Monday, do we?"

Though I know the car show isn't until next week, something tells me to confirm it, so I shake my head.

Something is very wrong. Mom prides herself on truthfulness. Why does she now need to lie to these people when it would be just as easy to say he's at the hardware store and due back any time?

"Pity to miss him."

"We'll, uh, we'll be sure to let him know you stopped by."

I don't know if it's the amulet's constant buzzing against my skin that irritates me or the fact that I just don't like these people—except Lorcan, of course. "I'm sorry, but you all are friends?"

"Shae!"

"No! It's obvious they didn't come to catch up. So, why are they really here?"

Brigid narrows her eyes at me, so this time I smile back, though a streak of adrenaline makes me warm.

Jarlath chuckles. "My, you've raised a sharp-eyed lass, Fae. You should be proud. Aye, we go way back. Rhode Island, was it?" Jarlath questions his wife but doesn't wait for confirmation before looking back at me. "Your parents lived next door. You weren't even a speck in your mam's eye back then."

"We had lots to talk about . . . those many warm nights," Brigid says as if it is a fond memory, but I don't believe it, with those dark beady eyes of hers she kept on my mom.

"Well, we were there for such a short time, so long ago." Mom glances at me, then back at Jarlath. Her

259

hand is shaky in mine. "I figured you'd moved back to Ireland ages ago."

"Not when business is to be had. Isn't that right, Brigid?"

"Ceart! You saps cheated us; lied to our faces, expectin' us to be done with it!" She stands up and leans a hand on the coffee table dividing us, her face beet red. "Rubbish as filthy as dirt, you be." Lorcan tugs at her, trying to get her to sit back down, but she shoves his hand off. "I said we'd be after ya. Claiming our pay."

"How dare you talk to her like that?" I say, suppressing the instinct to get up in her face. "You have no right to accuse her of—"

"Oh, it be the truth, Missy!" Brigid's eyes go ablaze. "Kept from ya all these years."

"Brigid, now, come back to me. Sit. No need for yellin'," Jarlath says, pulling on her arm until she sits down. He then whispers in her ear. She nods once, then glares hard at my mother while he says, "Long ago your parents—"

"Jarlath, no!"

"You would keep it from her still?" He leers at my mom. "Confess, Fae Donnelly, and make good on our bargain, or I be doin' it for ya."

A tear trickles down Mom's cheek as she shifts to face me but does not make eye contact. She sniffs and wipes the tears away.

"Mom, what is he talking about?"

Squeezing her eyes shut, she shakes her head. "I . . . I can't."

The room is silent. The stillness is as painful as a splinter in flesh.

"Your parents be askin' a favor," Jarlath continues. "We named terms. They accepted. Then once they received their wishes, they left in the night, debt unpaid."

"Mom, is that true?"

Using a tissue Jamie grabbed for her, Mom wipes her nose and face, then nods.

"Then pay them now, Mom! She'll pay you—"

"I will not!" she says through clenched teeth.

"Mom, just do it, then they'll leave."

"They tricked us!" she says, sounding nasally. "And convinced us it was the only way."

"Only way for what?"

"You knew the agreement. Agreed to it outright!" Jarlath says, tight-lipped.

"But I didn't understand what you wanted. Not really. And then I couldn't . . . I couldn't go through with it." She looks at me and holds my hand to her chest. "Not when I saw your sweet, beautiful, innocent face. I knew I could never do that to you!"

My heart pounds wildly; my mind spiraling out of control with crazy possibilities. "Do what to me, Mom?"

She bawls even harder.

A grumble comes up Jarlath's throat as he clears it. "They agreed for you to marry our firstborn, Lorcan."

Jamie and I gasp.

My mouth goes dry; my lungs are heavy as I exhale. "You . . . arranged my marriage?"

"Yes, but I knew it was a mistake. I had to stop it."

"Who would—how could they even—Wh-Why would you even agree to something like that in the first place? What did you ask them to do for you?"

"It's not—I-I can't tell you."

Standing up, I let my mother's hand fall. "It's so awful that you can't tell me, but you still agreed to pass me off to strangers for it anyway?"

"Shae, please, I—"

"And last night, you knew, didn't you?" I ask, glaring at Lorcan, who's still sitting unmoved and speechless.

"No, I—!"

"He's aware and has agreed to his fate," Jarlath says for him.

"You, on the other hand, have no choice in it." Brigid grunts.

"Excuse me? I do not consent to this; ever! Do you know how ridiculous you all sound? You can't make me marry your son!"

"Besides, Shae's already engaged, and it's definitely not to your son!" Jamie adds.

Jarlath and Brigid explode, screaming unintelligible things in their Gaelic tongue.

With hands fisted, Brigid grits her teeth. "I'm bleedin' raging! You dare wed her away?"

"Yes!" Mom shrills back. "She deserves to decide for herself."

"How dare you—" Brigid leaps from her seat and around the table.

My father, sprinting into the room from the kitchen, gets there first and blocks Mom, cowering on the couch. "What the hell is going on here?" His eyes expand when he sees Brigid's rage-filled face, and then Jarlath, rising to a stand across from him.

Gripping Dad's arm, Mom hoists herself up and hides behind him. "They're here for Shae!" she cries.

"The hell they are!" Dad snarls, his eyes darting from Brigid to Jarlath.

Jarlath takes a step around the table. "Now, Dale, you know we be havin' every right here!"

"You can take that deal and shove it!"

"Don't be daft! You know the consequences fur goin' back on your word," Brigid grunts.

Reaching out, Jarlath grabs his wife's arm and makes her step back to his side of the table. "Now, we're willin' to see past hidden, but marrying her off to another man. That be unforgivable, Dale!"

"Jarlath, it's her choice to make. Not ours. Not yours. We had no right to take it from her."

"You're a right eejit, Dale." Jarlath's hands ball into fists, his forearms bulging. He narrows his eyes at my father. "Make this right!" he yells.

"Jarlath, go home."

"No!"

"I mean it, get the hell out of my house. And if I ever see you anywhere near my family again—"

"This isn't over!" Jarlath huffs, glaring, then flinches when my dad steps toward him.

"Yeah, it is." Dad says and grabs Jarlath's arm, then shoves him toward the door. "You leave Shae alone. She's happy, and I won't have you mess that up!" Then he pushes him out the door, with Brigid hobbling after him.

Mom, Jamie, and I rush to the door, staying behind my father, standing tall in the doorway like a wall of protection. My heart swells with relief to see them now outside.

Jarlath staggers forward and then braces himself against the brick pillar by the stairs. Brigid tries to steady him, but he shushes her hand away. When he turns back around, his eyes hold a loathing that sends chills down my arms. "You're a right fool, Dale Donnelly. Shouldn't be messin' with things you don't understand."

"Better a fool who goes against you than a fool who tells his daughter who to love."

From behind, I hear a faint, "Shae."

Lorcan, having gone unnoticed during the commotion, is still sitting on the couch. He stands up and comes over.

In his eyes I see regret. The tense muscles in his sharp, square jaw soften when he stops in front of me. "Believe me, I didn't know it was you. Or that this would happen."

"I have no intentions of marrying you, Lorcan."

"Nor I you." His accent peeks through his voice.

"Then what did you think would happen coming here? That our families would reminisce and then go their separate ways?"

"I hoped that once they saw my betrothed and her family, they would realize how insane it would be to ask for such a thing and forget about it."

"You're dad's temper."

"I know, I'm so sorry, I—"

"Lorcan!" the raspy, gritty voice of his mother calls from outside.

"I'll make sure they leave you alone." He gives a weary smile and touches my shoulder, then goes down the hall. Stopping in front of my father, he says, somberly, "I'll keep them away."

"See to it that you do," Dad says and presses his lips together in a frown.

While Lorcan goes outside, Dad takes my crying mother back in. Jamie and I step out onto the porch. Stopping at the edge of the steps, we watch Lorcan help his father and mother into the car. He then goes around to the driver's side. Before getting in, he peers over the roof of the car at me. I give a slight wave back.

"Don't do that," Jamie warns, pushing my hand down.

"He's as much a victim in all this as I am, Jamie. He doesn't want this. His parents do. I have no reason to hate him just because they're crazy."

The car starts up and drives away, turning right at the end of the road. Though they are gone, I can't get the image of Jarlath's rigid, cold-as-ice eyes out of my head.

A hard lump of gut-wrenching angst sinks inside me, making me feel sick. Marcas was right. Trouble has found us yet again. I can't shake the feeling that this goes much deeper than an angry couple from Rhode Island hell-bent on keeping a ridiculous arrangement.

"That was insane," Jamie says, turning and leaning against the porch railing with her arms folded. "I've never seen your dad so mad."

While I stare down the empty street, I acknowledge her comment with a hum.

"What do you think the favor was?" Jamie asks as I think it.

"I don't know. Must have been huge, though, if they were desperate enough to take away my choice to marry for it." The notion makes my stomach turn. "Though I guess it explains my mom's relentless pursuit of finding me a husband. It was the only loophole she could find to stop it."

"Makes sense. You can't force a marriage if the person is already married."

"What were they thinking? That they would come and demand I marry Lorcan, and I'd just agree to it, or else they'd make me?" Conall pops into my head, and my blood runs cold. He tried; almost succeeded, too. But this is different. These are regular people. "I mean, what's the worst they could do? Sue my parents for breach of contract? What judge, in their right mind, would order such a fate on someone?"

Jamie snorts. "Yeah, good luck with that."

A chill of dread prickles up my spine, making the hairs on the back of my neck tingle as I wonder what the amulet has to do with all of this.

"You think Lorcan can keep them away?"

"They just spent the last twenty-one years searching for me. What do you think?"

"I'll call Finn—see where they're at." When I don't respond, she puts her hand on my shoulder. "Shae don't be gettin' all in your head about this. We'll

267

figure it out." Then she goes to the bench at the far end of the porch and makes the call.

My throat tightens as I try to fight tears of bitter frustration as I peer vacuously into the yard. The wind not only rustles my hair against my cheek but also the leaves in the trees around us.

We were so close. Two more weeks and all this would have been over. If they think I'm going to stop planning my wedding, they're idiots. Nothing is going to keep me from marrying Marcas in two weeks!

"They'll be here as soon as they can," Jamie relays, walking back to me. "Marcas wanted to know if you were okay. I told him you're hangin' in there."

Slowly, I nod and turn to her as the tears fall. She pulls me into a hug. "It'll be all right, Shae, I promise."

Squeezing her tight, I try to shut out the worry, but the knots still twist in my insides. Something about the timing of this seems almost intentional, as if the fates have one final challenge for us to overcome before Marcas and I unite forever. But if that is the case, and we fail, does that mean it's the end for us?

To be continued . . .

Thank you

for taking the time to read my books. I appreciate you and hope you enjoyed reading them as much as I did writing them. Stop by my website for access to more book-related fun, social media account access, newsletter sign-up, and much more. Then hit up the comment page and tell me more about what you loved about the books and why. I just love hearing all about it.

slmcmullin.weebly.com

SABOTAGE BY MIDNIGHT

the next installment in the

SECRETS BY MOONLIGHT SAGA

Release date: Summer 2025

STEPHANIE L. MCMULLIN

Stephanie resides in Utah with her husband and four children. *Secrets by Moonlight* was her first published work of fiction, followed by *Fate by Sunrise,* and *Deception by Nightfall.* Look for the exciting continuation of the saga in *Sabotage by Midnight* to be released in 2025.

Visit: slmcmullin.weebly.com for more details.

www.ingramcontent.com/pod-product-compliance
Lightning Source LLC
Chambersburg PA
CBHW020049180626
46812CB00006B/2254